D1071993

SHOOTOUT ON THE SABINE

Other westerns by Kent Conwell:

Llano River Valley
Grave for a Dead Gunfighter
Atascocita Gold
Junction Flats Drifter
Promise to a Dead Man
Bowie's Silver
Angelina Showdown
Gunfight at Frio Canyon
An Eye for an Eye
A Hanging in Hidetown
The Gambling Man
Red River Crossing
A Wagon Train for Brides
Friday's Station
Sidetrip to Sand Springs
The Alamo Trail
Blood Brothers
The Gold of Black Mountain
Glitter of Gold
The Ghost of Blue Bone Mesa
Texas Orphan Train
Painted Comanche Tree
Valley of Gold
Bumpo, Bill, and the Girls
Wild Rose Pass
Cattle Drive to Dodge

SHOOTOUT ON THE SABINE

•

Kent Conwell

AVALON BOOKS
NEW YORK

Published by Thomas Bouregy & Co., Inc.
160 Madison Avenue, New York, NY 10016

Library of Congress Cataloging-in-Publication Data

Conwell, Kent.
Shootout on the Sabine / Kent Conwell.
p. cm.
ISBN 978-0-8034-9981-2 (hardcover : acid-free paper)
1. Ranchers—Fiction. 2. Train robberies—Fiction.
3. Texas—Fiction. I. Title.

PS3553.0547S52 2009
813'.54—dc22

2009013017

PRINTED IN THE UNITED STATES OF AMERICA
ON ACID-FREE PAPER
BY HADDON CRAFTSMEN, BLOOMSBURG, PENNSYLVANIA

To my grandson, Mikey, and to Susan and
Mike, who by now are well aware
their lives will never be the same.

And to my wife, Gayle.

Chapter One

Behind a thin covering of gray clouds, the winter sun dropped slowly toward the towering crowns of the ancient loblolly pines and massive oaks beyond the Sabine River. Matt Fields studied the sky and shivered in his mackinaw. All signs pointed to snow—an unusual but not surprising occurrence in this part of Texas for late November. He sighed in resignation, reckoning it was about time someone swiped the silver-lining off the clouds that had been with him and Cotton for the last few weeks.

As the last wagon pulled up on the opposite shore downriver, he tugged his wide-brimmed Stetson down on his head and grimaced. He'd wanted to wait until morning to cross but the wagon boss, Ed Carson, insisted. "A few miles beyond the river is a prime spot to camp. Even got a small valley where we can loose herd the stock. Just you boys follow our trail. We'll hold over there a couple days. Maybe even celebrate Thanksgiving."

"You're the boss," Matt had replied with a nod, eyeing the crossing skeptically. Whenever he had pushed beeves across rivers he preferred a view upstream. Carson had picked a spot a hundred yards below a sharp bend. Not only did the bend block the view upriver, it created treacherous currents that could suck horses and beeves under.

When Matt and his partner, Cotton Wills, hired on in Westport Landing weeks earlier, he had an uneasy feeling about Carson and his bunch of wranglers. But that's all it was, a feeling, nothing he could put his teeth in.

With two thousand in gold coins in their saddlebags, he and Cotton were heading for Bastrop along the mighty Colorado River in central Texas to build a ranch. Since they were going in the same direction as the train, Cotton suggested they might as well pick up a few extra dollars. Besides, traveling with half a dozen wagons was a heap safer than two cowpokes crossing a wild country all by their lonesome.

"Hey!" The shout jerked Matt around. Over the bony backs of the small herd of cold-blooded beeves, his sidekick grinned at him. "Ready to push 'em across?"

"Might as well. Daylight's about gone. You take

the downriver side. I'll push 'em hard back here. Don't let any get past you. That blasted current will take them all the way down to the Gulf of Mexico."

With a brief nod, Cotton clicked his tongue and urged his pony forward. "Don't worry about me, partner." Suddenly, he sneezed and shook his head. "I knew I'd picked up a cold."

Matt grinned and squeezed his knees against the chest of his lineback dun, and the long-coupled pony eased forward, pushing the bellowing cows ahead of him.

Slowly, the herd entered the cold, muddy current. Immediately, the swift waters caught the skittish bovines and pushed them downriver.

On his sorrel, Cotton was swimming back and forth, waving his John B and yipping loudly in an effort to keep the swimming animals bunched.

Behind the herd, Matt whistled and called softly, not wanting to frighten the beeves, but well aware of the danger if they stopped swimming and started drifting with the current.

Every cattleman worth his salt used the river's current to help him push his beeves across. Instinctively, the cattle began swimming as they stepped into the current, which pushed the herd downstream. That was why the downriver wrangler was so important, to drive back any of the ornery bovines that tried to swim with the current.

Matt brought up the drag, his job not only to keep

pushing stock forward but to head off any frightened critters that tried to double back.

The icy water cut through cloth and flesh to the bone but in the hectic commotion of the moment neither cowpoke noticed.

Suddenly, Cotton waved at Matt and pointed upstream.

Matt glanced over his shoulder, and his blood ran cold. Lumbering around a bend was a huge tree, freshly toppled for the crown was thick with leaves.

In an instant, Matt knew they had gone too far to turn back. Their only chance was to drive the herd faster. With a shout, Matt whipped off his hat. "Whoeee! Get, cows, get!" At the same time, he knew it was of no use. Cows were so dumb they'd starve with only two inches of snow covering the ground. They couldn't realize the danger, and even if they did, they couldn't swim any faster.

The submerged tree slammed into the middle of the herd, breaking it apart and sending the spooked animals in every direction. By the time Matt and Cotton pushed the remainder ashore several minutes later, they'd lost half a dozen beeves.

Sitting on their ponies on shore with the remains of the herd milling about behind them, the two sodden cowpokes surveyed the river. "I don't see no sign of them, Matt."

"Me neither," the lanky cowpoke mumbled, his

gray eyes searching the roiling red water. With a shake of his head, he grumbled. "Let's get what's left up to camp, and I'll come back and look for the others."

Cotton muttered a curse. "I don't know why we should worry. They was nothing but culls anyway."

"Maybe so, but they belong to folks on the train."

"Reckon you're right. Still, I knew we should've waited until morning." He sneezed again as if to punctuate his remark.

From the time he was kidnapped by the Apache as a youth and sold to the Comanche to replace a boy who had been slain, Matt faced one hardship after another. If he'd taken time to think back over his life, the wiry man could have counted off dozens of times when he faced problems of more consequence than he now faced. He chuckled. "That tree could have come along in the morning just as well."

Sighing, Cotton removed his hat and ran his fingers through his light-colored hair. "Reckon so." He paused. "Why do you figure Carson was so all-fired anxious to cross tonight?"

Matt glanced at the leaden sky. "Probably worried about snow."

Cotton glanced at the thick clouds overhead. "A bit early, ain't it?"

With a grin, Matt shrugged. "Before the war, I saw one knee-deep about this time." He paused. "I reckon Carson has his reasons."

Lifting an eyebrow, Cotton grunted. "I still don't trust him. He's got sneaky eyes."

After running the stock into the small valley and leaving towheaded Lester Barlow and rail-thin Joe Hill, two of the young boys of the wagon train, to nighthawk them, Matt and Cotton returned to the bright, cheery fire in the middle of the circle of wagons.

George Barlow motioned the two over. He called to his daughter, who, to Matt's surprise, had donned boy's trousers. "Mary Elizabeth. Get these two soaking wet boys a cup of coffee."

She hesitated, eyeing the buckskins Matt wore. She'd heard gossip that he was part Indian. She shivered, wondering why the wagon boss hired a savage to ride with the train.

"Mary Elizabeth!"

"Yes, Pa." Dutifully, she poured the coffee, smiling at Cotton but frowning when she filled Matt's cup.

Ignoring her slight, Matt cupped the tin cup of steaming coffee in his hands. "Thank you, miss."

The slender woman placed the blackened pot in the coals. "You're welcome," she muttered without looking at him.

Matt glanced at Ed Carson who had come to stand beside them. He glanced at the arrowhead-shaped scar above Carson's right eye. "I reckon we've got another hour of light. I'll head back and see if I can pick up any of the other beeves."

"I'll go with you," Cotton said, rising to his feet.

Grinning at his partner, Matt shook his head. "No. You stay here and dry out. You been sneezing. You know how puny you are," he added with a teasing grin.

A taunting sneer played over Cotton's slender face. "You should be so puny."

Barlow nodded to Matt's clothes. "Best you dry out first."

Tossing his coffee grounds in the fire, Matt swung into his saddle and laid his hand on his thigh. "Buckskins dry fast." He paused and glanced at Mary Elizabeth who had her back to him. "That's why Indians wear them." He suppressed a grin when he saw her back stiffen.

Just as Matt wheeled his lineback dun around, Cotton called out, "Hey, partner. Hold on."

Expecting another wisecrack, Matt looked around. "Now what?"

The rail-thin cowpoke looked up at Matt somberly. "Be careful. You hear?" He glanced around at the darkening forest. "I got a funny feeling."

Matt laughed. "Probably a fish flopping around in your boot."

The cotton-topped cowpoke didn't smile. "I mean it, partner. Remember that night at Brown's Ferry on the Tennessee River outside of Chattanooga?"

A wry grin crossed Matt's face. How could he forget? Like all the other boys in butternut that November three years earlier, when he awakened that morning on

Missionary Ridge he was staring down at a mile-long line of Union soldiers dug in at the base of the ridge.

If he'd listened to his partner's ominous premonition the previous night, the two of them with their squad would have been back in Chattanooga. Instead, Matt caught a minié ball in the chest that laid him up for weeks, teetering on the razor's edge of death.

And all the time, Cotton stayed at his side. He never told Matt how he bribed for the assignment. Just after they were paroled at the end of the war, their sergeant confided that Cotton swapped his pearl-handled Walker Colt to a medical captain for the assignment.

Of course, Cotton denied it, swearing he had lost the revolver during the battle at Brown's Ferry.

Cotton prodded his partner. "You remember? About Chattanooga?"

Matt grew serious. "I remember. You had that same feeling the night before."

Cotton nodded. He laid his hand on Matt's arm. "I got the feeling something fierce now. You be careful."

Thick understory vegetation lined either side of the narrow trace that wound through the forest back to the river. Matt sat stiffly in his saddle, his eyes constantly scanning the forest around him.

The cold air crackled with the electricity of tension,

of the unknown. The deepening shadows among the silent pines cast fleeting images of skulking Indians, prowling jayhawkers, and furtive scalawags. The dun carried his head erect, his ears perked forward. Unconsciously, Matt flipped the loop off the hammer of his Colt.

Even before he came within sight of the boiling river, he heard the plaintive bellowing of the lost cattle. Uncoiling his latigo, he swung out a small loop, more to drive the stock than rope them. Best he could figure, there were six head missing.

"Easy, boy, easy," he whispered, gently guiding his dun with the slight pressure of his knees. At the river's shore, he spotted four head upriver standing at the water's edge staring at him.

In a singsong voice, he called out, "Sooo, bossy, bossy. Sooooo, bossy, bossy," as he walked his pony toward them, swinging into the shallows of the river to force the beeves back onto solid ground.

Two of the cantankerous bovines eyed him narrowly, their tails twitching like whips. Abruptly, they spun, and with a bellow, scampered back into the forest several feet before stopping and looking back.

Without warning, the popping of gunfire erupted from the direction of the camp. Matt jerked the dun around, staring over his back trail. The firing intensified.

He drove his spurs into the dun's flanks, and the

powerful animal leaped forward, racing down the shoreline for the trace.

In the next instant, a stunning blow struck his head, knocking him from the saddle and into the river.

Chapter Two

Wes Horrells leered with satisfaction when he saw the buckskinned cowpoke tumble backward over the rump of his dun and splash into the churning waters of the mighty Sabine River. He watched through narrowed eyes as the swift current pushed the limp cowboy downriver.

The smile on his bearded face grew wider. He swung into the saddle of his spavined horse and started pushing the cattle down the shoreline where he was to wait for Ed Carson and the rest of the boys. In the growing darkness, he failed to see the buckskin-clad body snag on a tumble of drift logs.

The cold water penetrated to the very marrow of Matt's bones, forcing him back to consciousness. He lay in the fork of a thick branch, the current tugging at his legs. His head throbbed. He laid his fingers on his forehead and discovered a knot the size of a pigeon egg. Another inch, half of his skull would have been floating down the muddy river.

Dragging his tongue over his lips, he blinked once or twice, but he could see nothing under the heavy overcast. He peered over his shoulder and spotted a faint glow reflecting off the belly of the thick clouds. Instinctively, he knew it was the wagon train.

As he started to pull himself along the thick bole of the sodden log, he felt the raft begin to shift. He stretched his arm behind him. His fingers touched nothing but water. At any time, however, he knew the swift waters could carry in another massive log, crushing him between them.

His head pounded. He felt his stomach churning. Despite the threatening nausea, he worked his way along the log until his feet touched bottom. Somehow, he managed to crawl ashore and collapse in the red mud, but not before the animal instinct for survival made him reach for his Navy Colt to make sure he had not lost it. His fingers touched the butt, and he sighed with relief.

All he wanted to do was sleep, but more than once during the war he had seen how head wounds could addle the senses of a jasper unless he forced his brain to function. Struggling to his feet, he squinted into the forest, focusing on the faint glow to the northwest.

With the coming of night, the temperature had fallen, and with it came the first flakes of snow. Confused thoughts tumbled about in his skull, but he knew instinctively to move upriver.

Despite stumbling over sodden branches and slogging through clinging mud, he kept his eyes on the faint glow glimmering through the straight black trunks of the pines. Minutes later, he found the trace up which the wagon train had journeyed, and along which he had pushed the beeves earlier.

That's when Matt smelled the odor of burning wood and canvas.

He hurried up the trace, each step sending shards of pain reverberating through his body, but with each step, the searing pain seemed to be clearing the confusion in his brain.

Through the stark black pines, the glow grew brighter. By the time he reached the edge of the clearing, the snow was falling faster. The lean cowpoke crouched behind a pine and shucked his six-gun and quickly replaced the primers with fresh ones. He muttered a silent prayer of thanks that he had used treated paper on his cartridges.

Two wagons still burned, casting a dim glow over the massacre scene. He grimaced. From the dim glow put off by the dying flames, he spotted the charred hulks of the remaining four wagons. Bodies were strewn around the camp like rag dolls. All of the livestock was missing except for one dead horse.

Matt's first impulse was to hurry into camp and see if anyone still lived, but his Comanche upbringing was too strong to ignore. He had to know what he was facing. If anyone was still alive, getting himself killed would not help them.

By now, the snow was beginning to cover the ground. From where Matt crouched, he could hear the hiss of the tiny flakes striking the smoldering wagons. He glanced up into the falling snow, hoping this storm would be a big one, big enough to keep everyone out of the forest.

Moving with the stealth of a preying mountain lion, Matt began circling the camp, studying it intently. Suddenly, he jerked to a halt when the flickering flames illumined a white Stetson on the ground beside a limp body.

"Cotton," he muttered, throwing caution aside and rushing across the clearing to the unmoving body. He grimaced. Half a dozen black holes caked with blood dotted the chest of his partner's mackinaw.

Matt knelt. Cotton's eyes were open. Though Matt could not see the dull film covering his partner's eyes, he knew Cotton was dead. He reached for Cotton's six-gun. It had not been fired. Matt's jaw hardened and his eyes grew steely. Cotton didn't have a chance. That meant whoever shot him was someone he knew, someone from whom he suspected no treachery.

Without warning, the crack of a rifle broke the silence, and a chunk of snow and mud exploded by his knee.

The wiry cowpoke lurched to his feet, grabbed his chest, and fell to the ground, his head facing the direction from which the shot had come. Cocked six-gun in hand, he lay motionless, his eyes barely open.

Several seconds passed, and then the murmur of voices drifted across the clearing. He could see nothing other than the falling snow.

The voices grew nearer. High-pitched, like children's.

Still, he remained motionless, his eyes almost shut. Moments later, a pair of black boots stopped beside him.

A boy's voice whispered, "Is he dead?"

Before anyone could answer, Matt swept his gun hand forward, knocking the feet out from whoever was wearing the black boots.

A woman's voice yelped, and a Yellowboy Henry flew through the air. Matt leaped to his feet, his teeth clenched.

And then he froze.

Looking up at him in terror were two boys bundled against the cold, and on the ground sat Mary Elizabeth Barlow.

One of the boys burst out crying, and the second exclaimed, "Please, don't shoot, mister. Don't shoot."

For a moment, Matt was speechless. Then he recognized the boys. They were the two who had been left to watch the herd. "What were you shooting at me for?"

The older boy gulped. "We thought you was one of them come back."

"Who?"

"Mr. Carson, the train boss. Him and his men started shooting everybody."

By now, Mary Elizabeth had climbed to her feet and was brushing the snow and mud from her trousers. She glared at him. "You didn't have to knock me down, you know."

Her tone rankled Matt but he ignored it. He had more important matters on his mind for the gunshot could have been heard for miles. He picked up the Yellowboy and handed it to Lester.

"We'll talk about that later. Right now, we've got to get out of here."

Mary Elizabeth frowned. "Why?"

"Because Carson and his men figure they killed everyone here. If any of them heard that gunshot they'll be back. They can't leave anyone alive as a witness. Now do you understand?"

She stared at him defiantly. "How do we know we can trust you? You're part Indian."

Matt groaned and shook his head. "Then don't trust me. Stay here and explain it to Carson." He looked at the two boys. "You going with me?"

For a moment, neither answered. Finally, each nodded.

"Good. Let's go." Matt glanced around, spotted a sheet of canvas burned around the edges, and quickly rolled it up. He gave it to Lester. "You carry this." Tearing off another strip of canvas, his hands flew as he wrapped it around a branch to fashion a small torch.

Lighting the torch, Matt headed out on the east trace, figuring that was the direction Carson had herded the stock and the direction from which they would be coming. In the darkness, their ponies would erase any tracks Matt's little party left.

Mary Elizabeth hesitated as the three moved out. She glanced around the clearing. The fires were burning low, and darkness was pushing in. Soon everything would be dark. After another moment of indecision, she hurried after them.

"Stay behind me," he cautioned them.

The snow grew heavier.

After only a few minutes, the wiry cowpoke spotted a fallen tree several yards off the road, an ancient oak toppled by the last storm. He led the small group from the road and into the forest. He grinned with satisfaction at the root ball of the tree. Snow covered the vines laced over the ball.

Holding the torch near the ball, Matt had the younger boy spread the canvas inside. "Now, climb in. It'll be crowded, but they'll never find us here." Mary Elizabeth hesitated until Matt added, "You three huddle together and pull the canvas around you. It will help against the cold."

Once the three were situated, Matt crawled beneath the vine-covered ball and squatted.

Five minutes later, the sound of hoofbeats reverberated through the air. Matt whispered, "Don't say a word."

Carrying two torches, the riders passed in the darkness, their voices muted by the snow.

Tulsa Jack rode around the camp, holding a torch high and scouring the ground at his feet. "I don't see no sign of nobody, Ed."

Ed Carson fixed Wes Horrells with a beady glare. "You right certain you killed that jasper at the river?"

Horrells gulped. Deathly afraid of Carson, he shivered. On more than one occasion he had witnessed his boss beat a man almost to death with his fists. "Yeah, Ed. He was dead. I ain't mistook about that." He nodded at the smoldering wagons. "Could be the fire set off a cartridge."

Carson studied the camp. "Well, that shot wasn't my imagination." He turned back to Horrells. "Wes. You stay here tonight. Back in the woods. See if anyone shows up. You hear?"

Horrells wanted to complain but when he looked at Carson's massive fists, he nodded. "Sure, Ed. Whatever you want."

After Carson rode out, Horrells found a snug hole

about a quarter-mile distant where he could roll out his bedroll and grab a few winks.

Matt relaxed as the riders rode back in the direction from which they had come.

"Are they gone now?" the younger boy whispered.

"Can't tell. Some might have stayed behind. Just try to stay warm and get some sleep."

After a few moments, the older boy muttered, "Mister. Is it true you're part Injun?"

Somewhere deep in the forest, a twig snapped.

Matt hissed. "Quiet."

Chapter Three

Next morning at first light, after warning the three to remain where they were, Matt left the shelter to scout the area. Beneath a sky of slate, the snow lay thick, covering all tracks. The air was still.

Casting out wide around the charred hulks of the wagons, Matt paused behind the scaly boles of loblolly pines to study the forest about him.

As a youth among the Penateka Comanche, he had learned patience by lying for hours over a rabbit hole waiting for the furry animal to emerge.

So now, he studied the forest with the same intensity and patience, waiting to see if a rabbit would emerge.

After an hour, all he had spotted were two deer.

Moving stealthily, he eased toward the camp several yards before pausing to crouch once again behind a cluster of leafless shrubs at the base of another pine.

Minutes dragged. A few random flakes of snow drifted to the ground. Movement to his right caught Matt's attention. A fox paused, lifted its head, then darted into a warren of briars.

From behind, a light breeze brushed the back of his neck. Suddenly, somewhere far to his left came the whinny of a horse. Matt dropped lower into his crouch behind the tangle of shrubs.

His rabbit had appeared.

Wes Horrells looked over his shoulder in the direction of his horse and muttered a soft curse. He had been curled in his soogan beside a fallen tree and had gained a modicum of warmth in the last few hours. His horse whinnied again. Cursing, he climbed from his bedroll. He'd wait another hour, and then if he saw no one, he'd return to camp. Carson couldn't fault him for that.

When Horrells struggled to his feet, Matt spotted him. A slow grin spread over his rugged face. He had suspected as much. He leaned a shoulder against the pine and waited.

An hour later, he watched silently as the owlhoot rode away. Had Matt been alone, he would not have hesitated to take the man's life, but he had three children to look after. Well, he reminded himself wryly, two children and a spoiled young woman.

The snow continued to fall.

Before Matt had covered a mile, a single gunshot broke the silence of the snow-covered forest. The wiry cowpoke ducked behind a loblolly and waited.

After several minutes, he moved out, anxious to reach the small sanctuary beneath the ball of tree roots. He paused when he spotted several butternut trees, in the middle of which was an ancient butternut that had been dead for several years. He guessed it was probably ten or fifteen feet wide, and no telling how old. Probably a seedling centuries before the first Spanish and French explorers set foot on the continent. The long, angular branches were covered with snow. At the base of the tree was an opening. An idea hit Matt. He peered inside and shook his head. Not enough room for the four of them.

He looked around, searching for shelter from the weather, which appeared to be growing more intense. To the east, he spotted a small hill, and near the crest lay a tangle of snow-covered trees, probably uprooted by a tornado years before. The dead limbs of their crowns had long broken off.

Quickly, he hurried through the pines to the fallen trees, hoping for at least a temporary refuge for the coming night.

He paused beside a butternut tree on the edge of a

gully on the side of the hill. To his surprise, the trees had fallen across the deep gully. Over the years, vines had covered the trunks and fallen to the bed of the gully. A thin blanket of snow covered the vines.

Matt glanced over his shoulder, then slid down the side of the gully. Shucking his six-gun, he pulled the vines apart and peered beneath the trees. In the dim light, he saw there was enough room to walk upright, and on the far wall of red earth was a cave. Hastily he searched in the gloom. The cave was spacious enough for a small fire, the Indian way, and their soogans. With a little work, they could make the cave a snug refuge until he could figure out how to get them back to civilization.

Back outside, he clambered to the top of the hill. Similar pine- and oak-covered hills rolled to the north. This would be a good spot. Any smoke would be caught by air rising from below and swept away.

He grinned. Finally, luck had decided to sit on their shoulders.

Snow was falling briskly when he reached their temporary shelter. "Quick. We've got work to do."

Mary Elizabeth frowned from inside the crude shelter. "What kind of work?"

Matt snorted. "The stay-alive kind. First, we're going back to the wagons to see what we can salvage. Then I've found us a place to hole up in for as long as we need." He rolled the canvas and looked at one young boy. "What did you say your name was, button?"

Mary Elizabeth spoke up. "He's my brother. Lester Barlow."

The older boy said, "I'm Joe Hill."

A frown knit Matt's brow. "You boys were nighthawking the herd when the scavengers hit, weren't you?"

Lester nodded. "Yes sir, Mr. Fields."

"All right." He glanced over his shoulder. The snow continued to fall. "We've got to move fast before the snow stops. Joe. You carry the rifle. Lester, you carry the canvas. Now, let's go. And be quiet. I think those riders are gone but we can't take the chance. There might be one or two left around."

When they reached the clearing, Mary Elizabeth hesitated, her eyes staring at the snow-covered hulks of the burned wagons and the smaller mounds beneath which lay the dead. Matt recognized her apprehension. "Don't worry. We'll come back and bury them, but first we've got to make Carson think he killed everyone."

She shook her head slowly and backed away a few steps. "I can't go in there."

Matt felt a flush of sympathy. "Just wait. We'll do what's needed."

Mary Elizabeth remained on the outskirts of the

clearing while Matt and the boys salvaged more canvas, a few cooking utensils, tools including an axe and a shovel—both with charred handles—clothing, lanterns, and a few food staples the fire had not consumed nor the snow ruined.

Matt dug through the snow where he had seen Cotton leave his saddle and saddlebags. A wave of elation surged through him when he found the saddlebags for they contained powder and lead for cartridges. His elation was shortlived for the saddlebags containing his and Cotton's two thousand in gold was gone.

He laid his hand on the moneybelt around his waist. All he had was seventy odd dollars to his name.

Moving in single file with Matt in the lead, the small group hurried through the forest to the windfall.

Joe whistled when he peered through the opening in the wall of vines. "This is larger than our cabin back in Kentucky," he muttered. Without warning, tears filled his eyes. He scrubbed balled fists at them roughly.

Mary Elizabeth drew her heavy coat about her shoulders tighter. She eyed the darkness beneath the trees with misgiving. "What about snakes?"

Over his shoulder, Matt replied, "Hibernating." He winked at Joe who was carrying supplies inside. "All we have to worry about are bears."

The young woman gasped, and Joe suppressed a grin.

The gully was five or six long strides across, fifteen or so feet to the cave. Matt drove a branch into the wall of the cave on which to hang the lantern. He looked around at Joe and Lester. "I'll hang canvas across the mouth of the cave and get some wood for a fire. Bring in the rest of the gear. Put your blankets in the cave. We'll arrange it all later."

Lester frowned up at him when he saw Matt's hands were empty. "Ain't you taking the axe?"

"Not today." He hooked a thumb over his shoulder. "Too much noise. Can't tell who might be around. We've got to play our hand close to our vest for a couple days."

Dead trees littered the forest floor, many falling apart at the touch, worthless as firewood. Others were still hard but brittle enough to break although they would quickly burn. He paused every few moments to study the silent forest through the thick flakes drifting to the ground.

That night, they slept on canvas spread over the damp floor of the cave. Near the mouth of the cave, a small fire sent tiny flames licking at the darkness above. Smoke drifted across the ceiling and out the opening at the top of the canvas, then broke into wispy tendrils as it dissipated into the trees.

Fortunately, the small cave was roomy enough that Matt could drape a canvas sheet in front of Mary

Elizabeth's bed, offering the young woman a bit of privacy. For the first time since he had made her acquaintance, she smiled at him.

Next morning, Matt was up before the sun, prowling the silent forest made even more silent by the blanket of snow. He discovered a few animal trails in the snow and deftly built snares for the smaller animals.

Limbs sagged under the weight of the snow and ice. From deep in the forest, snapping limbs echoed through the pine and oak like gunshots. He paused when he reached the clearing in which the massacre had taken place, eyeing the mounds of snow heaped over the charred ruins of the wagons. He winced in anguish when he saw the smaller mounds had been disturbed by animals.

Overhead, ominous gray clouds scudded over the treetops, their snow-filled bellies scraping the sharp tops of the great loblollies. He set his jaw, and his gray eyes grew hard and cold. Despite the chance of discovery, he would return later that day and bury the dead.

Having cast about the forest in a five-mile circle, he swung by the snares he had built that morning. A faint smile played over his lips when he spotted the rabbit dangling from a snare. With practiced moves, he split the small animal down the belly and tossed the entrails on the snow. From above, two sparrows and a bluejay swept in on the viscera.

He grinned at them and dropped the rabbit in the game bag about his waist.

Rawhide-tough and lean as dried leather, Matt turned back toward the cave. He moved according to the instincts pounded into him as a youth with the Penateka Comanche—always remaining scant moments from cover, never venturing into the open, always blending his silhouette into the background.

Suddenly he froze, his eyes fixed on a dark object sprawled beneath a cutbank of a small creek. Like a wraith, he faded into the wild azalea near a loblolly. Knowing his silhouette was effectively hidden, he studied the figure, quickly realizing it was a man.

He waited but the man did not move.

Easing forward, Matt shucked his Navy Colt, hoping there would be no reason to use it. In the snow-enhanced silence, the reverberating echo of a gunshot could travel for miles.

His eyes narrowed when he recognized the figure as Indian.

He moved closer, careful to slide his feet to avoid the cracking of the snow's crust. When he was fewer than five yards from the unmoving Indian, Matt slipped behind a pine and lobbed a chunk of wood at the inert figure.

The man didn't move; then Matt spotted the bloody hole in the Indian's back. He glanced over his shoulder, his gray eyes quartering the deep and dark forest about him. He remembered the single gunshot he had heard the day before.

He studied the still figure again, noting impressions in the mud that suggested the Indian had dragged himself beneath the bank out of the weather.

A foot or so beyond his outstretched fingers lay an Osage orange bow and a quiver with only two arrows. Flexing his fingers about the grip of the Colt, Matt eased forward, touching his toe to the still body.

A moan broke from the man's lips.

Taking no chances, Matt slipped the Indian's knife and tomahawk under his own belt before kneeling. With one hand, he turned the unconscious man over.

The man's eyes flickered.

Matt took in the Indian's dress from the beaded moccasins to the long tuft of hair in the middle of his head. Looked like a Caddo. He whispered, "English. You speak English?"

The unconscious man didn't respond.

Opening the Caddo's deerskin shirt, Matt studied the exit hole about three inches below the collarbone. There had been little bleeding. The wound appeared healthy. The cold obviously had delayed the infection. More than once, Matt had witnessed the preservative effects of cold on wounds, so he was not surprised to observe the condition of this one.

Pulling the unconscious man to his feet, Matt

swung him over his shoulder. He retrieved the Indian's bow and quiver from the snow, then set out for the cave.

Suddenly, he froze, peering in the direction of the river. He tilted his chin, sniffing the air. There it was again—woodsmoke.

He muttered a curse. The smoke was not from his camp in the cave because the breeze, any breeze, carried the smoke from the crest of the hill into the crown of the forest so the heavy winds could blow it away.

No, this smoke came from another's fire.

His blood ran cold.

Ed Carson!

Chapter Four

With the grace of an antelope, Matt moved quickly, carrying the unconscious Indian back to the cave. He kept his fingers crossed, hoping the jostling and bouncing of his lope would not trigger a hemorrhage of the man's wound.

Forty-five minutes later, Matt spotted their sanctuary. He paused, sniffing the air. He had been right. The smell of smoke was not from their camp, but from another's.

As soon as he tended the unconscious man, he would find out just who was camped at the other fire.

Mary Elizabeth gasped when Matt pushed through the canvas drape. The two young boys' eyes grew wide. Matt ignored them as he placed the unconscious man on his pallet. Over his shoulder, he said, "Boil some snow. I need hot water."

The young woman stood transfixed. "But—but that's an Indian."

Matt shot her a sharp look, then glanced at Lester. "He's Caddo. Now, fill one of those pots with snow and put it on the fire."

Lester nodded. "Yes, sir."

He handed Mary Elizabeth the rabbit. "Can you skin this?"

She nodded. "Certainly."

"Good. Skin and quarter it. When we finish with the water, toss it in. We'll have rabbit stew tonight."

Joe stepped forward, his eyes wide. "Can—can I help with anything?"

Matt shook his head, wishing for some medicine to stop the infection. For a moment, he studied the slack features of the unconscious Indian and gave a faint grin. He slipped his knife from the scabbard and handed it to the young boy. "Go outside and bring me back a handful of bark from that tree on the edge of the gully."

Joe frowned at Mary Elizabeth, shrugged, and ducked out through the canvas. At that moment, Lester returned and placed the pot on the fire.

Matt stripped the man's buckskin shirt and with the warm water, gently bathed the wound, noting with satisfaction the bullet had exited the wound just below the shoulder.

Despite her apprehension, Mary Elizabeth found herself drawn hypnotically to Matt's ministrations to the swarthy Indian.

When Joe returned with the slivers of butternut bark, Matt poured water into another pot and dumped the bark in it. He set it on a flat rock on the edge of the fire.

Lester frowned up at him. "What's that for?"

He gave Mary Elizabeth an amused look, then turned to Lester. "Old Indian remedy. Remember it. The bark is from a white walnut, what the old-timers call butternuts. Boil the bark down to a syrup, and it heals wounds." He paused to stir the boiling bark with the tip of his knife. "I don't know what's in it but I've never seen it fail."

Joe shook his head slowly and whistled. "I didn't know Indians knew stuff like that. I figured it was only the white man who had medicines that cured different sicknesses and all."

While he tended the wound with the butternut syrup, Matt replied, "No. The Indian has his own medicines. You ever have a stomachache from eating too many green apples?"

Lester chuckled. "I sure have. Mary Elizabeth too."

The young woman blushed. "Lester! You know better than that."

Matt continued, "You know what a dandelion is?"

"Yeah. That little plant with a white head that you can blow into the air."

"That's the seed head. Boil the roots and you have a potion that will cure any stomachache." Finally, Matt sat back on his heels and studied the motionless man before him. He glanced over his shoulder in the direction of the other camp. While he was anxious to see who made it, he didn't want to leave until the Indian awakened.

He studied the slumbering brave closely, noting the black hair cut about three or four inches long except in the middle where the topknot was at least a foot long. Matt grunted. The unconscious man most likely was Caddo. He picked up the bow and quiver of arrows. The bow was of Osage orange, what some called bois d'arc. The arrow shafts were of willow.

Matt pursed his lips, turning the arrow shaft over and over in his hands, studying it. Willow. That made sense. Willows were prevalent along rivers, the preferred habitat of the Caddo.

Joe cleared his throat. "What are you looking at, Mr. Fields?"

The lean cowpoke glanced up. "Call me Matt, okay?"

Joe nodded enthusiastically. "All right, Matt."

Matt held up the arrow. "I'm trying to figure out what tribe he's from. I'm almost certain he's Caddo. They live along rivers and ponds, and that's where willows grow." He held up the arrow. "This arrow is made from willow."

A tiny frown knit Joe's brow. "Is that the only tribe around?"

Continuing to study the arrow, Matt replied, "No. From what I picked up the last few weeks, the Tonkawa is south of us, the Wichitas back to the northwest."

Joe's frown deepened. "You mean, we got Indians all around us, huh?"

With a chuckle, Matt nodded. "Looks that way."

By now, the rabbit stew was beginning to boil.

"Mmm. Smells good, sis," muttered Lester, patting his stomach.

A faint blush colored Mary Elizabeth's cheeks. She shot a hasty glance at Matt and ran her fingers through her long hair in an effort to untangle it, a move that was not lost on the lean cowpoke, nor was the frustrated stamping of her foot at the futility of straightening her hair. She nodded to the stew. "I put some flour in to thicken it but it would be better if we had potatoes."

Matt grinned. "Next time we will. I'll show you and the boys how to find wild potatoes."

At that moment, the unconscious Caddo moaned, and his eyes fluttered open, then grew wide with fear when he saw the white man looking down at him. He started to rise, but Matt held him down gently with one hand while making the Northern Indian sign for the word "friend" with his other hand—two fingers in front of his neck, facing out and up.

Some of the fear left the warrior's eyes, replaced with curiosity. He glanced at the other white-eyes staring at him. Then Matt hooked his forefingers together in front of his chest, the Southern Indian sign for friend.

With a brief nod, the Indian relaxed. "I friend."

Matt chuckled and glanced at Mary Elizabeth. "He speaks English."

"Good English. From the missionaries. I Charley One-Horse."

"All right, Charley," Matt said. "We need to get something down you. Build up your strength."

Charley shook his head.

Matt insisted. "A few bites at least." He managed to spoon a few gulps of rabbit stew between Charley's lips before the exhausted Caddo fell asleep.

Before he did, he revealed he was a Hasinais Caddo who had been sent by his father, a Hasinais chief, on a peace mission to the Tonkawas back to the south. When Matt asked who shot him, Charley replied, "I not know. I see no one."

Matt put himself around a bowl of rabbit stew, surprised to find that it was good. He nodded to the young woman. "This is right tasty, miss."

She blushed.

He nodded to the sleeping Caddo. "He is nothing to be afraid of. We saved his life, and he will always be indebted to us. That's how they are, so if he wakes up while I'm gone, don't worry."

Mary Elizabeth frowned in alarm. "Gone? Where are you going?"

He tied the quiver to his belt and swung the bow over his shoulder. "When I ran across Charley One-Horse, I smelled woodsmoke back toward the river. I want to see who it is. Just you stay here. Keep the fire small, and Joe, you keep that Yellowboy Henry close. I don't expect any trouble but you never can tell."

He turned to leave, but she stopped him. "What about . . . about those back at the wagon train?"

He studied the three. They were holding up well given their youth although he figured he was only four or five years older than Mary Elizabeth. Of course, he reminded himself, in real living, he was probably twenty years her senior.

"I'll take care of them," he answered, reaching for the axe and shovel. "It'll be after dark when I get back, so don't get spooky, you hear?"

The three nodded.

Matt suppressed a grin when he saw Joe's Adam's apple bobbing up and down.

Outside, the snow had begun falling once again.

Moving effortlessly, Matt swung by the wagon train and dropped off the tools before continuing toward the river. Alert as a preying panther, he constantly tested the air, well aware that the thick stands of pine and oak and gum twisted the tenuous currents of air in every direction.

The pungent odor of woodsmoke was not as heavy as it had been earlier. He glanced at the sky, the internal clock of his Comanche youth telling him there were two or three hours before dark.

He cut northeast off the trace, planning on striking the river well above where they had pushed the beeves across. For a moment, he lost his concentration when he remembered the crossing with Cotton. Had it been only a couple or so days earlier? It seemed like a month.

His eyes narrowed as he realized his and Cotton's dreams of building a ranch in the lush valleys of central Texas were now nothing but wispy tendrils of hope that had gone up in smoke.

From the thick forest ahead echoed the roar of the Sabine River in its headlong rush down to the Gulf of Mexico.

Remaining just inside the tree line, Matt crept downriver.

The snow grew heavier.

Ahead, Matt spotted movement. He froze, then slowly dropped into a crouch behind the scaly bark of a giant loblolly.

Just inside the tree line some fifty feet downriver, smoke drifted upward from a tiny fire. Two cowpokes were moving about, a redheaded one with a smallpox-scarred face saddling his pony and the other pouring coffee grounds on the fire.

Matt's eyes turned to ice when he recognized Wes Horrells and the pockmarked face of Pink Higgins, two of Carson's right-hand men. His eyes studied the forest about him carefully, looking for Tulsa Jack, Blacky Dow, and Ed Carson, but finally he was satisfied that the two scavengers were the only ones in camp.

Horrells looked up at Higgins, who swung into the saddle and huddled down in a worn Yankee greatcoat. "I reckon Ed'll have to be satisfied that there ain't no one else around here except that Injun we kilt."

Higgins grunted. "Saddle up. I'm cold and hungry waiting here for you. Tulsa Jack is downriver. I want to get back on down to Sabine Town before Ed gives away my share of the loot. I still think he had something up his sleeve by having us spend an extra night here."

"Yeah." Horrells cackled. "How much gold do you reckon was on that train?"

Higgins shrugged. "Tulsa Jack said almost eight thousand."

Eight thousand in gold! Hot blood pounded in Matt's ears, and a great roaring of anger filled his head. Eight thousand—two thousand of which was his and Cotton's gold! The other six must have come from the wagon train.

Quickly, he nocked an arrow and let it fly at Higgins.

Chapter Five

At that moment, Wes Horrells doused the fire with water, and luckily for Higgins, his cow-hocked bay crow-hopped at the sudden hissing. The arrow drove through the heavy coat sleeve and into his left arm instead of severing his spine as Matt intended.

Higgins screamed. The bay reared, then bolted downriver.

Horrells looked around in panic. Ignoring his gear, he leaped on the bare back of his speckled roan and dug his spurs into the animal's flanks.

Matt cursed his own flush of anger; but remembering Higgins' remark about meeting up with Tulsa Jack Neal, he hurried into the abruptly deserted camp to salvage what he could.

Horrells' saddlebags contained a half-full bottle of Old Crow whiskey, a box of Sharps cartridges, and a pair of dirty long johns that Matt immediately tossed into the river.

From the worn saddle, Matt pulled out a battered but serviceable Sharps and a grass lariat.

He paused to study the now empty camp. On the ground lay Horrells' soogan, probably thick with fleas. A good washing and smoking with sweetgum and pennyroyal would clean it up. The blankets and canvas would come in handy.

A sudden gust of snow reminded him he had much to do before returning to the cave.

A mile downriver, Tulsa Jack Neal grabbed his six-gun and ducked away from the fire when he heard approaching hoofbeats. Peering around the trunk of an ancient oak, he saw Pink Higgins racing down the shoreline, mud and snow flying from his pony's hooves. A frown twisted Neal's hatchet face when he spotted the arrow bobbing up and down in Higgins' arm.

His anguished face pale as the falling snow, Higgins yanked his bay to a sliding halt by the fire and half climbed and half stumbled from the saddle.

Neal holstered his six-gun and hurried to meet his partner. "What the Sam Hill?" he muttered, eyeing the arrow in his partner's arm.

Clenching his teeth and shaking his head, Higgins groaned. "Blasted Injun. Wes said he was deader than a can of corned beef."

"What Injun?" Neal frowned, doing nothing to aid the moaning outlaw.

Grimacing, Higgins turned his arm to Jack. "The one Wes claimed he kilt. Yank this out."

Neal grinned at the pain evident on Higgins' face. "Sure, Pink. Sure. Just hold on. You're lucky it went clean through." He shook his head, and with a taunting grin added, "Be a shame if that arrowhead come off inside your arm. I heard of one old boy that lost his whole arm when he got infected like that."

"Just do it," Higgins groaned.

With the swift, deft moves of a proven gunfighter, Neal snapped the head from the arrow and jerked the shaft from Higgins' arm.

Higgins screamed. "Blast, Jack. You almost tore off my arm."

Neal laughed and fetched a bottle of whiskey from his saddlebags. "Here. Shuck that coat and wash your arm off with this and take a couple of swallows. It'll make you feel better."

About that time, Horrells rode up.

Neal shook his head in disbelief. "Where's your gear?"

Horrells slid off his roan and took the bottle from

Higgins. "Back there, and I ain't going back for it." He took a long gulp of whiskey and shivered.

Taking the bottle from Horrells, Neal knocked down a couple of hefty slugs. "So what happened?"

Horrells shook his head and drew the back of his hand across his lips. "Best I can figure, a whole passel of Injuns come after us after we kilt that one."

Higgins tore a strip from the bottom of his shirt and handed it to Horrells. "Here. Tie this around my arm, and don't say we. You was the one." With a sneer on his pockmarked face, Higgins spoke to Neal. "He claimed he kilt one yesterday. He said nobody would miss an Injun. Besides, he hadn't kilt one in over a year, he said." Horrells snorted and jerked the bandage tight, causing Higgins to yelp. "Be careful, you hear?"

With a sneer, Horrells asked, "You want to do it yourself?"

Neal arched an eyebrow and slid the whiskey back in the saddlebags. "Stop the arguing. Let's get us on down to Sabine Town and our share of the loot."

Horrells protested. "I don't know why Ed wanted to go on down to Sabine Town. We coulda stopped in Coy's Landing or at Pendleton's Trading Post."

Higgins growled. "Me, I'm riding on in to Sabine Town. You can stop and see that little filly at Pendleton's if you want."

"Yeah." Neal sneered.

For a moment, Horrells considered doing just that, but when he looked into the encroaching darkness in the forest he knew he would be riding on with them.

Just before dark the clouds blew away. It was the dark of the moon, but the starlight reflecting off the pristine snow provided enough light to read by and more than enough to bury by.

Matt buried all the bodies in a common grave, dragged heavy timbers over them, and sprinkled coal oil over it all to keep the animals away. Remembering Mary Elizabeth's frustration trying to untangle her hair, Matt searched through the rubble for a comb, but found none.

It was early morning before Matt pushed through the canvas drape that served as a door. Charley One-Horse sat up when Matt ducked in, eyeing the Sharps and coil of rope. Matt leaned the Osage orange bow against the wall. "Shoots well," he said. "You make good arrows."

The Caddo nodded briefly. "Good willow."

From behind the canvas drape, Mary Elizabeth whispered, "There's still some stew left."

"Good. Tomorrow, we'll bring in some meat."

Charley frowned. "Heavy snow tomorrow."

Matt hesitated. "You sure?"

The Caddo nodded, his face solemn. "Pretty so. Our spirits have said this is the Winter of the Great Ice."

Pursing his lips, Matt studied Charley. He wasn't about to dispute the Caddo's observation, for several times during his years with the Comanche he had witnessed weather phenomenon no one could predict except the medicine man. He gestured to the outside. "We got a right big heap of it now."

"Yes. There be more."

Matt nodded, remembering knee-deep snows that drifted higher than his head. "Then I reckon come morning we need to get things ready."

The next morning while they squatted around the small fire chewing on flour cakes baked on rocks facing the flames, Mary Elizabeth asked, "What are we going to do now? Our families are gone. I don't know about Joe, but Lester and me are all that's left. We've no kin anywhere."

Joe shrugged. "I don't know if I got kin or not."

Matt and Charley exchanged knowing looks. Matt cleared his throat. "As long as we're here, we're safe. Charley says this will be a bad winter. Nearest town I know of is Sabine Town. That's probably where Carson is holed up. I don't plan on taking you youngsters anywhere near him."

Mary Elizabeth bristled. "I'll have you know, I'm not a child, *Mr.* Fields."

A patient smile played over Matt's lips. "No, miss. You most certainly are not, and that's another reason I don't want you around him and that bunch of hardcases he hangs with." He paused. "While burying your folks, I found a few more items we can use. Some blankets made it through the fire, and a few other things."

He turned to Charley. "You up to setting out snares?"

Charley nodded.

"Good. Les, you and Joe come with me to the clearing and haul back the goods. I'll try to get us some venison."

Joe glanced at the Sharps in Matt's hand. "What about the noise? Them Sharps are mighty loud."

Matt gave him a crooked grin. "I got a feeling those old boys last night didn't stop until they got to Sabine Town. It's a chance but we need meat. Besides, I plan on hunting a few miles to the southwest."

Lester and Joe hesitated when they reached the clearing where the massacre had taken place. Matt pointed out the mass grave, then led them to a windfall under which he had stacked several blankets, canvas, and the leather traces and chains that had survived the fire.

Lester frowned up at Matt as he shouldered the traces and chains. "What good are these?"

Matt looked around. "If we're going to be out here as long as it now looks, we need everything we can get our hands on. Now, you boys haul that back to camp, and give Charley a hand skinning any game.

And if you have time, take the axe and haul in more firewood. Understand?"

The boys nodded as one. They watched in silence as Matt, without another word, turned and disappeared into the forest.

After a moment, Lester gulped. "This is scary out here all by ourselves."

Joe swallowed hard, then patted the Yellowboy. "That's all right. We can take care of what we have to do. Now, let's get all this stuff back to camp."

Lester hesitated, staring at the mass grave. Joe looked around. "What's the matter?"

The younger boy pulled his wool coat tighter about his thin shoulders. "I just can't believe all of this has happened to us in the last two or three days." He looked up at the older boy, his eyes red-rimmed. "Why, just last week, we—"

"That was last week, Lester. This is today, and you and me have got to do whatever we need to stay alive. Understand?"

The younger boy nodded slowly. "Yeah, but I'm still scared, Joe. Real scared."

Joe forced a grin. "Me too. But if we do what Matt says, we'll be all right."

Chapter Six

Charley One-Horse predicted correctly. Just after dark, a heavy storm slammed into the forest. An hour later, Matt staggered in, two haunches of venison slung over his shoulder.

He paused to savor the comfort of their refuge. The cave was cozy and warm, and the frying rabbit and baking biscuits filled the interior with succulent aromas.

He dropped the unskinned haunches on the floor. "I hung the rest of the carcass in a hickory about two miles out. If the snow's too deep tomorrow, we'll rig some snow shoes to bring it in."

Lester glanced at his sister then looked up at Matt. "What happens if we get snowed in?"

Charley nodded to three bundles of tightly bound

branches about three feet long. "Today, I find willows. I show white boys to make arrows."

That night after Mary Elizabeth and the two boys slumbered, Matt told Charley that he had run across bear sign not far from the cave.

Charley grumbled. "Bad. Bear should be sleeping. Always, they mean." He shook his head. "Big trouble when bear wakes in middle of sleep."

"We'll warn the others in the morning."

In the Wild River Saloon, Ed Carson leaned back in his chair and stretched his legs toward the red-bellied wood stove. The heat of the rot-gut whiskey in his stomach and the warmth radiating from the stove should have put him in an expansive mood, but instead he glowered at the thick snowflakes striking and momentarily sticking to the window before sliding down, leaving a moist trail. Absently, he ran his finger over the blood-red scar above his eye.

At his side sat George Dow, a swarthy Louisianan from the bayous around New Orleans. His curly black hair earned him the nickname "Blacky." Devil-quick with a six-gun, he was twice as fast with a stiletto. In New Orleans, he made a comfortable living using his knife to remove individuals on contract.

After a few years of furtive murders, the upright citizens, many of whom had once been clients of the man, forced him to flee the city-that-care-forgot or dangle on the gallows in the middle of the French Quarter. His choice.

Dow glanced at his boss. "There is trouble, yes?"

Carson snorted. His black eyes remained fixed on the window. "Someone, maybe more than one, escaped the train." He turned to the smaller man. "And that someone could get us all hanged."

The swarthy man wanted to sneer but he knew Carson too well; he had witnessed the big man's violence and he wanted no part of it. "But, it was the Indian that put the arrow in Pink, no?"

Tossing down the remainder of his whiskey, Carson pursed his thick lips. His three-day-old beard stood out darkly against his weathered skin. Of his four men, he listened to Dow most, not that he had a great deal of respect for the Louisianan's opinion, but that he had even less respect for those of the other three. "You think so?"

"*Oui*. What else?"

His eyes narrowed as he studied the smaller man. "I don't know, but that's what I aim to find out."

Dow wanted to laugh. The weather was too fierce to do anything but remain inside and drink good whiskey. He suppressed his smile. "*Oui*. Whatever you say." He gulped the rest of his whiskey and reached for the bottle on the floor by his chair. He shrugged. Noncommittally, he added, "But, *mon ami*, the weather, she is very bad."

Carson extended his glass. As the smaller man

filled it, Carson said, “As soon as the weather breaks, we’re going back.”

The next morning dawned bright and clear, not a cloud in the sky. Birds of the forest welcomed the new day with gay songs. The faint gobble-gobble of wild turkey drifted from the depths of the thick forest.

Charley One-Horse eyed the blue skies then ducked back inside. He grunted. “Good weather.” He held up three fingers. “Two, three days no snow.”

Over breakfast, Matt told the others of the bear.

Lester’s face paled. “What if he tries to come in here?”

Joe threw his shoulders back and nodded to the Yellowboy and Sharps leaning against the wall. “We’ve got the rifles. They’ll stop him.”

Charley grunted and pointed to the fire. “Throw burning fire. He run.”

Matt cautioned. “Important thing is, when you’re outside, keep your eyes open. Don’t go out by yourself.”

To Matt’s dismay, he cut bear sign less than a mile from the tree. With stoic fatalism, he knew it was only a matter of time before they faced the hungry beast.

He walked faster, anxious to retrieve the venison. He had a feeling they were going to need it.

* * *

Back in Sabine Town, Ed Carson, bundled in a fur-lined leather coat and his broad-brimmed hat tugged down over his ears, led his small band north along the undisturbed snow-covered trace that paralleled the muddy river. He muttered a curse that he was getting such a late start but he was the only one to blame. He'd had too much whiskey the night before.

The night before. He grinned. For a few moments the night before, he thought he might have to kill Neal for the gunman insisted on splitting the eight thousand dollars. Carson refused, stating no one would get a share if he did not help finish the job. And as far as he was concerned, as long as one person survived the massacre, the job was still unfinished.

Reluctantly, Neal backed off. His eyes narrowed. He'd bide his time, and then, he promised himself, he'd take the whole pot.

As the band of killers entered the forest, traveling proved easier as the trees grew so thick that the depth of the snow was less beneath the canopy of leaves than in open vales.

Pink Higgins winced as the irregular gait of his pony jostled his arm. The scars from his youthful siege of smallpox stood out on his pale face.

Wes Horrells brought up the drag. He called out, "We ought to reach Pendleton's Trading Post by noon, don't you reckon, Ed?"

Neal snorted. "Probably, but we ain't going to

have no time for you to look up that little filly you're so lollygagged about."

The smaller man started to argue but Carson snapped, "You two shut up. We ain't stopping at Pendleton's unless it starts snowing again. We'll lay over tonight at Coy's Landing. We'll headquarter there until all of this is done."

Dow wanted to argue that a single arrow was no indication of anyone surviving the attack on the wagon train but he kept his mouth shut. Carson had it in his head that a survivor had shot the arrow. He knew Carson well enough to know that until the grizzled killer spent a week or more scouring the countryside and finding nothing, he wouldn't be satisfied.

That was a small price to pay for his share of the loot, Dow told himself.

Mid-morning, Matt reached the venison cached high overhead. From the four-toed pugmarks in the snow, he saw the smell had drawn wolves and bobcats, the latter being discerned by the lack of claw marks on the toes.

He grinned when he spotted claw marks on the tree and imagined the frustration of the bobcat when the animal couldn't reach the cached venison dangling from the overhead limb.

His blood ran cold when he spotted the five-toed pugmarks of the bear. He studied the tracks, noting that the bear seemed to be favoring his right front for the imprints were much lighter than the other three feet. He studied them a moment longer, seeing the right foot had no claws.

He searched the dark forest around him. The bear was not too large, maybe two hundred pounds and two and a half feet at the shoulder, but with an injured foot he was going to be as salty as Lot's wife.

Quickly, he lowered the venison and threw it over his shoulder. Though it weighed a solid seventy-five pounds, he moved effortlessly, his sharp eyes continually scanning the forest about him.

On impulse, he swung by the clearing. He smiled to himself. The coal oil he had spread over the mass grave kept the bear from tearing it apart as the beast had done to many of the burned hulks while scavenging for food.

A few hundred yards farther on, he grimaced when he spotted the pugmarks of the bear. The beast must be mighty hungry to travel such a distance.

Matt hung the venison in a butternut tree about fifty yards from the camp. While sipping some cassina tea brewed from the roasted leaves and stems of yaupon holly, Matt and Charley made plans for the bear.

Her face drawn in apprehension, Mary Elizabeth asked, "Will he come here?"

For a long moment, Matt studied her, then nodded. "Sure as we're sitting here. Probably tonight." Lester gasped but Matt continued, "That's where we have the advantage. We know he's coming."

Joe spoke up. "Then let's just shoot him. We've got the Henry and the Sharps."

Charley One-Horse gave Matt a knowing grin. Matt explained. "Normally, I'd say yes. But keep in mind, there's a heap of jaspers out there who want to see us dead. Now maybe they're just over the hill, or maybe they're all the way down to the Gulf of Mexico." He fixed the young boy with a challenging look. "You want to chance which one?"

Joe's ears burned. He shook his head. "No, sir. Not me."

Matt chuckled. "Smart boy. I don't either, so we'll face our visitor here."

Lester gulped. "But how?"

Charley grunted. "We have fire." He glanced beyond the mouth of the cave.

Matt followed the warrior's eyes to the vine-covered logs over the gully. He nodded. "If we build one out there, the whole shebang will go up in flames."

The Caddo grunted. "Use fire in cave."

"Right. We'll make a couple of lances. I've never seen a creature, man or beast, that can face fire and lances without turning tail."

"But won't he come back?"

His face firm but his eyes understanding, Matt nodded. "By then we'll have more time to get ready for him. All we have to do is scare him away tonight."

Chapter Seven

As darkness settled over the vast forest, Ed Carson reined up at the hitch rail in front of Coy's Landing, a weathered clapboard building that served not only as one of the northernmost ports on the Sabine, but also as a saloon, café, livery, and hotel.

Several miles to the northwest through the great pine and oak forest, Matt and Charley took one last look around outside before settling in for the night. Inside the cave, water boiled on the fire and four hardwood lances, sharpened to a needlepoint and fire-hardened, leaned against the wall. Beside the fire, three torches lay ready, their canvas heads soaked in coal oil.

Matt and Charley waited outside. The night was clear. Around midnight the waxing moon rose, lighting the forest in a soft glow. Trees stood out in stark relief against the brilliance of the white snow.

From time to time, dark creatures darted through the forest, rabbits fleeing, wolves pursuing. From somewhere in the distant darkness, a rabbit shrieked, and moments later the beating of an owl's wings once again broke the silence.

Charley grunted.

Matt looked around, and the Caddo indicated a slow-moving shadow lumbering through the forest in their direction. A cold chill ran down Matt's spine. He ran his tongue over his dry lips. "There he is."

The Caddo grunted.

Matt eyed the approaching beast. He had guessed right. The animal was about five feet from tail to head and a tad over two feet at the shoulder. He walked with a pronounced limp.

From time to time, the bear stopped to sniff, dig in the snow, but always continuing inexorably toward the cave. When he was fewer than thirty feet distant, Charley and Matt slipped down the bank and under the fallen trees.

They heard the crunch of the animal's paws on the crusted snow.

"He's coming down," Matt whispered. "Let's get inside."

Each of the boys stood by a pot of boiling water, their hands wrapped in canvas against the heat. Mary

Elizabeth waited behind them, a torch in each hand and ready to light them as soon as the boys threw the water.

From beyond the canvas covering the mouth of the cave came the soft snuffling of the beast as he followed the scent of the humans.

Lester glanced up at Matt, his eyes wide, his face pale.

"Bear smell us," Charley said.

Joe and Lester nodded, each leaning a little closer to his pot of boiling water. Lester licked his lips.

Without warning the canvas fluttered, and then the black bear stuck his head inside.

In the next instant, two pots of boiling water soaked his head, and two lances drove deep into either side of his neck just ahead of the muscular shoulders.

With a startled grunt the creature lurched back, and bawling in pain disappeared into the night, ripping off much of the thick vines that hung from the dead trees to the floor of the gully.

Mary Elizabeth held the unlit torches expectantly.

One side of Matt's lips ticked up. "I don't think we'll need them tonight."

Joe chuckled, and Lester joined in.

Their mirth faded when Matt added, "To be on the safe side, Charley and me will take turns watching until morning."

Throughout the remainder of the night, they could hear the bear prowling the woods around the camp, bellowing and snarling.

"What do you think?" Matt gestured to the sound.

Charley chuckled. "No more tonight. That one, he is trying to build up his nerve."

Matt chuckled. "He'll get it back. That one is hungry, and he knows there's plenty of grub around here," he said wryly.

"Tomorrow maybe. Tomorrow night, he come."

The Caddo was right. The bear remained in the forest for the remainder of the night, circling the gully.

Despite their victory the night before, the boys were silent around the breakfast fire. Mary Elizabeth voiced their concern. "He'll be back?"

Matt sipped his hot sweet fern tea. "You can bet on it, but we're going to stack the deck in our favor." He glanced at Charley, who grinned back at him.

At Coy's Landing back to the southeast, Carson and his four gunhands moved out, following the narrow trace along the river's edge. The big man rolled his massive shoulders. Once and for all he would satisfy himself that no one had survived the sneak attack on the train. The snow would make for easy tracking, and if the crippled old drunk swamping out the saloon back at the landing knew what he was talking about, there were a couple of days of good weather ahead.

As soon as they finished a breakfast of flour cakes, fried venison, and honey that Charley had stolen from a nearby bee tree, Matt led them to a tall pine he had discovered a half-mile from their camp. Near the base of the tree, the pine had snapped like a matchstick. It had fallen onto a smaller pine that had bent almost double supporting the heavier tree.

Matt gestured to the tree and looked at Charley. "This one is heavy enough to do the job."

Charley studied it impassively. With a grunt, he said, "We bait tree." He turned to the boys. "Bring dead branches. Many." He indicated the bowed trunk of the smaller pine. "I cut at it."

The boys glanced at Matt, obviously puzzled by Charley's plan. Matt explained. "A deadfall. We hang bait from the smaller tree. When the bear pulls on it, the big tree will fall on him." He paused and grinned sheepishly at Mary Elizabeth. "If we're lucky." He paused again and cautioned the boys. "Don't go near the clearing, We can't take a chance on Carson showing up and spotting any tracks."

Joe frowned. "You really think Carson will come back for us?"

Matt studied him soberly. "We can put a noose around his neck. What do you think?" He turned to

Mary Elizabeth. "You wait here with Charley and the boys."

A trace of alarm flickered in her eyes. "Where are you going?"

"Back to camp to get some bait. I figure a forequarter of venison will be enough to tempt our friend."

She shot Charley another hasty glance. "If you don't mind, I'd like to go with you. I've been inside so much the last few days, I'd like to stretch my limbs some more."

With a shrug, Matt headed over their back trail. "Fine with me. Let's go."

During the thirty-minute trek to camp, Matt learned that the Barlows had sold their farm in Tennessee and were bound for the Colorado River down below La Grange.

Flexing his fingers about the pistol grip of the Sharps, Matt kept his eyes moving, probing the depths of the forest. "Family down there?"

The young woman had removed her bonnet, and her dark hair spilled out on the shoulders of her heavy wool coat. "No. Papa was an orphan, and Mama's kin back in Tennessee are all passed away. Some kind of sickness took the community. Mama had a sister and my granny. They all died. Papa, he just wanted to start fresh. Good land down in Texas, he said."

Matt glanced at her from the corner of his eyes, thinking just how much they had in common. That had been the reason for his journey, to build a ranch. Suddenly, he froze, then grabbed Mary Elizabeth's arm and pulled her into a crouch.

She turned to him but he hushed her with his finger to his lips. He nodded to their right. She gasped when she spotted the lithe cougar gliding through the forest. They were downwind so he had not smelled them.

The young woman nodded to the Sharps but Matt shook his head briefly. "He isn't hurting us, not yet."

Without warning, the cougar paused, then dropped to the snow, its long tail slowly sweeping back and forth.

Mary Elizabeth leaned closer to Matt and whispered, "What does he see?"

The lean cowpoke could smell the freshness of her skin. For a moment he didn't answer.

"Huh?" She looked up at him.

"What? Oh. Over there. Look."

Ahead of the motionless cougar was movement in the shadows of the forest. Moments later, an antlered deer emerged, head high, searching for danger.

Mary Elizabeth caught her breath, mesmerized by the life-and-death scene playing out before her very eyes. For long seconds, the two creatures remained frozen like stone.

Without warning, the deer spun and bounded into the forest. At the same time, the cougar exploded in a thirty-foot leap, and in the next instant, was swallowed up by the forest.

For the next few seconds, the sounds of the chase echoed through the shadows of the pine and oak until the only sounds were the singing of snowbirds.

She looked up at him, a frown knitting her brows. "Did he catch the deer?"

Matt shook his head, thinking how the scene was so similar to the dynamics between his small party and Ed Carson. "The cougar is fast and strong but he doesn't have the endurance of a deer. If he doesn't get his prey within the first hundred yards, he's out of luck."

She broke into a satisfied smile. And for the first time since Matt had met her, he realized just how pretty she was.

By the time they returned with the forequarter, Charley had fashioned a fence of sorts from the dried branches and limbs to force the bear into a loosely confined space below the deadfall.

He had hacked at the bowed trunk of the supporting tree so that a slight tug would snap the slender trunk and send the large pine crashing to the ground.

Matt eyed the trap with appreciation. It was a crude deadfall, but given the tools with which they had to work it was as effective as they could construct on short notice.

Tying two of the leather traces together, Charley fastened one end around the forequarter and hurled it over the small pine, letting the venison hang down to within about six feet of the ground.

Joe whispered to Matt, "You figure it'll work?"

"More than likely. The bear's hungry. Once he grabs hold of that venison, he won't let go." He nodded to the circle of dead limbs and branches. "If he stays in there, chances are good that pine will do the job."

Charley looped the other end of the leather trace about the trunk of a nearby pine and knotted it securely. He stepped back. "Now we wait."

Mary Elizabeth gasped when she spotted a small bloodstain on Charley's buckskin vest. "You're bleeding!"

The Caddo laid his leathery hand on the fresh stain. "It is no trouble."

Matt frowned. "You sure?"

With a faint smile, Charley nodded, his topknot bobbing. "Yes. Now, you go. I stay."

Chapter Eight

Matt glanced around the forest. "I don't like leaving you here by yourself but this is no place for the youngsters."

With a grunt, the Caddo had pointed to a nearby tree with a three-pronged fork about twenty feet above the snow-covered forest floor.

Lester frowned. "What if he comes after you? Bears can climb trees, I've been told."

"Not this one. Bad foot, no claws." He laid his hand on the tomahawk hanging from the sash about his waist. "I have this."

Back at the cave, Matt stirred up the banked fire and slipped a pot of sweet fern tea in the coals. Soon the interior was warm and cozy. Lester kept glancing at Matt. Finally, unable to contain himself any longer, the young man blurted out, "Can I go outside and wait? I know I can't see nothing but I'd feel better just watching."

Matt glanced at Mary Elizabeth, who was smiling at her little brother. "I don't know why not." He looked at Joe. "You want to watch with him?"

Joe jumped to his feet. "I sure do."

"All right, but take your lances and don't go far from the cave, you hear?"

After the boys left, Matt poured some tea and leaned against the wall of the cave. He slipped a willow branch from one of the bundles Charley had harvested and began peeling the bark.

A tiny frown knit the young woman's face. "What are you doing?"

Matt continued peeling the willow branch. Without looking up, he explained. "Making arrows. After the branches dry, the first step is to peel them, then straighten any curves in the shafts."

Growing curious, she crossed her legs and squatted beside the fire. She stared at the slight curve in the willow shaft. "Straighten them? How do you do that?"

With a crooked grin, Matt chuckled. "Like this."

After peeling the last of the bark, he nudged a hot stone from the fire with the toe of his boot. Applying gentle pressure on either end of the shaft, he rubbed the slight curve against the hot rock, and gradually, the curve straightened. He held it up to her. "That's how."

Her eyes grew wide. "I didn't know you could straighten wood like that. How did you learn all that? With the Ind—" She stopped abruptly, her ears and cheeks burning. "I, ah . . ."

Matt's gray eyes danced in amusement. "With the Indians. The Comanche to be exact. Don't be embarrassed. Those were some of the best years of my life."

Her frown grew deeper. "But, what about your parents? What—I mean—"

He shrugged and continued working to straighten the shaft. "Murdered by the Apache. They stole me and sold me to the Comanche." He paused and glanced at the canvas drape serving as a door, wondering about Charley.

She shivered. "That must have been terrible."

With a crooked grin, he looked up from his task. "For a boy, it wasn't all that bad. Like I said. They were pretty good years. Hunt, fish, ride. The women and girls did all the work." He shook his head. "No, ma'am, it wasn't all that bad. White man might learn a thing or two from the Indian along that line," he added with a mischievous grin.

Her cheeks colored, and a tiny smile played over her heart-shaped lips. "You're teasing me."

He laughed. "Maybe a little, but it's good to see you smile. You probably don't know it, but the Indian believes that laughter is what keeps a soul alive. They claim when you laugh, spirits fill your body with young blood, taking the years from you."

She studied him suspiciously. "You don't believe that."

Matt shrugged. "About the spirits? No, but I do know that laughter sheds the body of bad thoughts, and it's those bad thoughts that cause some folks to sink lower and lower until they climb into their grave."

She shrugged. "I can't argue that." She reached for a willow shaft. "Mind if I help?"

Time flew as they peeled willow bark.

Without warning, the canvas door flew open, and Lester barged in. "Charley's coming."

They hurried out to meet the Caddo.

Matt glanced at the clouds moving in. The day was almost gone. "I was beginning to wonder about you."

Joe burst out, "What about the trap? Did we get the bear, huh?"

Charley shrugged. "He not dead. He run into woods. He busted up heap bad. Howl like papoose. Leave trail of blood."

A frown wrinkled Matt's forehead. "He coming back?"

The Caddo's black eyes grew even blacker, blacker than the pools of stained water hidden deep in the swamps along the river. "Me, I think not." He gestured to the forest around them. "No more this his hunting ground."

Lester cleared his throat. "How does it know that?"

Charley eyed the small boy somberly. "Enemies here strong. He go where they weak."

"But," Matt cautioned them, "that doesn't mean we get careless. Understand? In fact, we are going to rig up some sort of barrier just in case one of his friends starts snooping around."

Deep in the forest, the injured bear growled and snapped at the new pain throbbing in his chest. Ragged coughs racked his body, spraying the pristine snow with a fine spray of red blood.

The heavy pine had struck him solidly. Had it not been for his injured right front leg giving way, causing him to roll to that side, the pine would have snapped his spine, killing him almost instantly. Instead, the impact broke several ribs, driving the slivered ends into his lungs.

As the pain intensified, so did the beast's rage, a blind fury that would erupt on the first creature to confront the bear. As night settled in, he wandered the forest, his frustration and his rage increasing with each painful step.

Later, his black eyes, glazed with excruciating anguish, glimpsed a distant light in the darkness.

Less than a mile distant, Ed Carson and his band of four scavengers had set up camp after their ride from Coy's Landing. The large man was well on his way to drinking himself to sleep in front of the fire.

Wes Horrells glanced at the overcast sky. "Reckon we ought to spread a fly against snow, Ed?"

Carson growled, "Ain't supposed to be none. Just throw the canvas over your head and go to sleep. Leave me alone." His head resting on his saddle and his legs stretched out toward the fire, Carson tilted the bottle of whiskey to his lips and gulped another few swallows. He had begun having second thoughts about the arrow. Perhaps his boys were right. An Injun had shot Wes. Still, he couldn't shake the feeling that someone had survived the massacre.

Of the five hardcases, the only one not addled by whiskey was Tulsa Jack Neal. He lay in his soogan some distance from the fire, studying the others, sneering at their drunkenness. On the far side of the fire, Pink Higgins and Blacky Dow snored, sleeping the sleep of the dead drunk. Horrells was close to joining them as was their boss, Carson.

Ever since they pulled out of Coy's Landing that morning, Neal had toyed with the idea of leaving the other four dead in the middle of the forest and riding off to New Orleans with eight thousand dollars in gold. He grimaced. He should have kept the two thousand he found in the dead cowpoke's saddlebags instead of giving it to Carson, who put it with the six thousand from the wagon train.

But soon, he told himself, real soon, he'd have it all.

Unlike most killers, Neal was clever, always careful to leave no sign behind to identify himself. If he had allowed himself the vanity to notch his handle for every cowpoke he planted, the handles would be nothing but slivers of wood.

But such flamboyance always garnered attention, and such recognition was something Neal carefully avoided. That was the very reason he had never been arrested. In fact, he had never even had a finger pointed at him.

Through narrowed eyes, he studied the camp. Absently, he rolled a Bull Durham cigarette and touched a match to it. Taking a deep drag, he blew a stream of smoke into the frigid air.

From deep in the forest, a branch snapped.

Neal glanced over his shoulder into the darkness then shrugged. Whatever it was, the fire would keep them away.

With the cigarette dangling from his lips, he slipped his hand under his blanket and eased his six-gun from the holster. His fingers danced lightly over the cool metal he had come to love and that he knew as well as the back of his hand.

Carson first, then Horrells. The other two were so drunk, dynamite wouldn't awaken them. He smiled grimly. Another few minutes. *As soon as I finish my cigarette,* he told himself.

Horrells began snoring. Neal flipped his cigarette into the fire. It was time. Slowly, he rose to his feet.

He narrowed his eyes and swung his six-gun around onto the sleeping form of Carson.

Behind him came a soft growl.

With a frown, he glanced around, squinting into the darkness.

Without warning, an ear-splitting roar ripped apart the silence of the night, and two hundred and fifty pounds of rage and fury leaped from the darkness into the light.

Neal managed a chilling shriek before a set of five hooked claws ripped across his face. For a moment, Neal's body, frozen in shock, stood, then collapsed as the savage bear, berserk with pain, grabbed Neal's shoulder and shook him like a doll.

The drunken cowpokes staggered to their feet, befuddled by the commotion. When the bear spotted Higgins and Dow stumbling around, he charged them. "Bear, bear, bear!" Higgins screamed, turning and darting into the night, making only a few feet before he straddled a pine and knocked himself unconscious.

Carson and Horrells, even as they backed away, were firing slug after slug into the black furry coat of the rampaging bear that had turned on Dow.

The bear swung Dow to the ground. All that saved the startled jasper was his heavy coat and the fact he pulled it up above his head.

The growling bear slapped at Dow then turned on Horrells and Carson, who had retrieved his Winchester 66 and was pumping slug after slug into the animal.

As suddenly as the bear attacked, he dropped to the blood-covered snow, blood leaking from over a dozen wounds.

Carson stood frozen, staring at the beast. His hands began to shake and he grabbed his bottle of whiskey.

Off in the woods, a branch snapped.

As one, the men drew closer about the fire, guns ready and their eyes on the encroaching darkness.

Horrells muttered, "What about Jack?"

Carson snorted. "What about him? He's dead, ain't he?"

Dow looked around, blood running down his skull from the ripped flesh. "W-where's Pink?"

"Go look for him if you're that worried," Carson snarled. "Me, I'm staying by this fire."

Chapter Nine

The popping of gunfire jerked Matt and Charley awake. Slipping into his boots, Matt hurried outside, pausing to loosen the knots holding a lattice of hickory branches they had fashioned to serve as a barrier in front of the canvas.

While a creature with the strength of the black bear could easily shatter the door, doing so would create enough commotion so those inside would have sufficient time to grab their rifles.

Outside, the gunfire had died away.

Matt frowned at Charley. "What do you think?"

Matt was surprised to see the Caddo smile. "The bear. He find someone."

The cowpoke nodded. "Carson maybe?"

"Carson maybe."

"Then, come morning, let us see."

Suddenly, two more shots rang out.

Charley frowned at Matt, the question in his dark eyes.

"No idea," Matt replied.

The three terrified hardcases huddled around the fire until morning, taking care to keep it blazing. From time to time, Horrells, who boasted the mental capacity of a three-year-old, fired into the dead bear.

Carson snarled. "What the Sam Hill you doing that for? That animal's dead, sure enough."

"I just want to be sure."

With a disgusted shake of his head, Carson snapped. "Save them slugs. That one just might have a mate around somewhere."

The smaller owlhoot froze, such an idea never having surfaced in his brain. His watery eyes swept the dark forest, and he dragged his tongue over his dried lips.

Slowly the three relaxed. The bear was dead, and false dawn had begun graying the dark sky.

His Colt in hand, Carson eased forward, studying the dead beast. He arched an eyebrow when he spotted the raw flesh on one side of the animal's snout and the tiny blisters among the remaining patches of hair.

He cut his black eyes to the forest and nodded tersely. Someone was out there. Of that he was certain. Suddenly, a branch in the forest cracked. As one, the three turned on the noise, six-guns pointed in the direction of the sound.

Horrells grinned when he saw Higgins stagger from behind an ancient loblolly pine, the skin split open on a knot on his forehead, and a dried stream of blood caked on his bewhiskered face and grimy greatcoat. His eyes were already starting to turn black.

Carson stared into the shadows beyond Higgins, his black eyes struggling to penetrate the gloom of the forest and the identity of those in the shadows. He scratched at the heavy beard on his rock jaw, and a faint sneer played over his lips. *Whoever is out there,* he swore to himself, *I'll find you.*

From behind a windfall not far from the camp, Matt and Charley watched as the four rustled up their gear and swung into their saddles. One reached for a lead rope on an unsaddled pony, but the animal broke loose and disappeared into the forest as the disgusted cowpokes hurled harsh curses after it.

Moments later, the four huddled, then two turned back to the river while Carson and Horrells continued west up the narrow trace.

Charley indicated he would follow Higgins and Dow. Matt followed Carson and Horrells.

Moving as silently as a stalking wolf, Matt trailed the big man and his partner, sensing they were heading to the site of the massacre.

Sure enough, a few minutes later, the two owlhoots

reined up and studied the snow-covered lumps in the clearing.

Standing in his stirrups, Horrells frowned, puzzled. "Something don't look right, Ed."

Carson thought the same thing. "What makes you say that?"

Shaking his head slowly, the owlhoot said, "I don't know. When we come back the first time, it seemed like there was more wagons." He shrugged. " 'Course, the snow makes it all look different, don't it?"

Without replying, Carson dismounted and kicked the snow from one of the burned hulks. When he spotted claw marks in the charred wood, he chuckled.

Horrells shifted in his saddle, glancing anxiously over his shoulder. "What is it, Ed?"

"Nothing." He surveyed the clearing. "Reckon the bear tore the wagons apart. That's why it looks a heap different. Animals took care of the bodies. Them what was left will be gone come spring thaw."

The smaller owlhoot sighed with relief. "Reckon we're heading back to Coy's Landing now for the split, huh, Ed, huh?"

Carson swung into the saddle. "Reckon."

Horrells chuckled. "I got plans already for my share."

Carson cut his eyes at the smaller man. A soft growl from the dark forest momentarily froze him. He laid his hand on the butt of his Colt. His cold black eyes squinted into the thick shadows, seeing nothing.

Every muscle tense, Matt froze, staring into the yellow eyes of a crouching cougar not twelve feet from him. Though the animal was just as surprised as Matt, it instinctively dropped into a preying crouch, its muscles bunched, its long tail swishing back and forth slowly, its cold yellow eyes fixed on the man creature before him.

Matt held his breath as he and the cougar remained motionless for several long seconds. Without warning, the cougar scuttled a few inches closer.

From experience, Matt knew the animal was setting up a charge. The forward movement was a test, to see the reaction of the prey. If the beast's prey turned and ran, he charged. If he did nothing, the lithe animal scuttled forward another few inches.

Matt gathered himself.

Seconds later, the cougar made another forward move. Matt yanked his hat from his head and swung it at the cougar, at the same time unlimbering the Colt at his side and lunging forward.

Startled, the lithe lion bounced aside several feet, then turned and growled, his tail whipping from side to side.

Matt raised his six-gun and lined the muzzle on the cougar's forehead. Long seconds passed, and without warning, the animal turned and vanished into the forest.

Keeping his eyes on the shadows into which the

beast had disappeared, Matt leaned back against the scaly bark of a pine and sighed with relief.

Moments later, a light snow began to fall.

During the ride back to the warm refuge of the river port, Carson tried to convince himself that his imagination had gotten the best of him, that there was no one back in the forest. Yet, how could a jasper explain the burns on the bear's snout? He didn't build a fire himself and stick his nose in it.

No. Someone was out there. Perhaps the Indians who put an arrow through Higgins' arm. Or perhaps a lone survivor of the wagon train who could put a noose around his neck!

Back at the owlhoots' camp, Matt paused for a moment only when he discovered Tulsa Jack Neal's body. The dead man's saddle remained but his saddle gun had been taken. All they left was a lariat, which Matt threw over his shoulder. Leaving the dead man where he lay, Matt quickly skinned the bear and headed back to camp. The skin would make a heavy door, for the wind gusting down the gully constantly whipped the heavy Onasburg canvas about.

From time to time, Matt caught a wispy tendril of woodsmoke, enough to arouse the curiosity of a seasoned woodsman, but one so tenuous that the average traveler would never notice. He grunted in satisfaction.

Back at the cave, the boys hit him with a barrage of questions as he gobbled down flour cakes and venison smothered with honey. He grinned up at Mary Elizabeth as he gulped down a swallow of cassina tea. The liquid was strong, strong enough to keep a body from sleep if enough were taken in.

She smiled shyly.

By the time Charley One-Horse returned, Matt and the boys had fleshed the hide and strung it over the lattice framework, fashioning a thick door against the bitter weather.

Charley studied the door and nodded. "Good. Keep out wind." He nodded toward the river. "Those I follow go to the place called Coy's Landing."

Matt peered in the direction of the river port. Remembering the expression on Ed Carson's face as the rugged outlaw studied the scene of the massacre, Matt sensed that Carson figured someone had survived.

So, what was his move after reaching Coy's Landing? Would he split the eight thousand and head for Galveston and then some foreign port, or would he continue his search for the survivors?

The Caddo's eyes flickered as he caught the expression on his friend's face.

That night around the fire, the conversation turned to home, and memories of past Christmases. Eyes welled with tears.

Pouring another tin cup of cassina, Matt turned

to Mary Elizabeth. "What is today, do you reckon? I know the month is December."

Lester and Joe frowned at each other as the young woman concentrated. She cleared her throat. "We've been here a spell. We crossed the Sabine around the end of November. I remember Pa saying that"—her voice choked—"Pa saying—"

Quickly changing the subject, Matt looked around at Charley. "You know what I think?" he said exuberantly. "I think it might be just a week or so until Christmas."

Charley frowned. "Chris-mas? What is Chris-mas?"

Young Joe looked at the puzzled Caddo in disbelief. "You don't know what Christmas is? Why, it's one of the most fun times of the year. All kinds of goodies to eat."

"Yes," Lester chimed in. "And sometimes, if you're good, you get a gift."

Mary Elizabeth arched an eyebrow at her little brother. "And if you're bad, you get a bundle of switches."

Lester's grin sagged into a gloomy frown.

She laughed and hugged him to her. "Don't worry, little brother. You don't deserve switches this year. Maybe Santa Claus will slip a nice present under your bed."

"Yeah," Joe said, joining in the gaiety. "And we'll sing Christmas songs like 'The First Noel' and 'O Come All Ye Faithful.' "

Lester laughed. "I like 'Away in a Manger.' "

Charley frowned. Matt shrugged. "Never heard of them."

Mary Elizabeth laughed. "I bet if you heard them, you'd remember." And she broke into the first verse of 'The First Nowell.' Her voice was clear as sweet spring water. Lester and Joe joined in.

After the first verse, Mary Elizabeth laughed, her cheeks flushed. "Now, you sing along with us."

Matt laughed. "We'll try, but my voice is more suited to stray cows than Christmas songs."

For the next hour, the dark forest around the gully tree resonated with the strains of joyful music and laughter. For the first time in weeks, the last month's tragedies were forgotten, at least for the moment.

As the small fire burned low that night, Matt said, "So, do we celebrate Christmas this year?"

Lester frowned. "But we don't know when it is."

"Then let's set a time. We been here several days. I reckon it could be another week or so. That's time enough to make ready. We'll have our own Christmas dinner."

Mary Elizabeth beamed. "I think that's a wonderful idea."

"Yeah," Lester said.

Chapter Ten

As the gray of false dawn crawled across the morning sky, Matt and Charley One-Horse stepped out into the bitter cold. The snow had ceased, leaving several inches on the ground.

The Caddo whispered, "You go Coy's Landing?"

Pulling the collar of his mackinaw around his neck and tugging his John B down on his head, Matt grunted. "My partner and me saved two thousand dollars in gold coin. We planned to build us a ranch out on the other side of Bastrop. Carson killed my partner and took the gold. I reckon on getting it back."

Charley nodded briefly. He laid his hand on the handle of his knife. "I will go with you."

"No." Matt nodded to the cave behind the Caddo. "You stay here and look after them."

"Then take the Sharps."

Matt held up a lariat in one hand and patted his holstered six-gun with the other. "This is all I'll need."

The Caddo grunted. "Watch for the Tonkawa to the south."

With a crooked grin, Matt glanced at the gray sky above. "Maybe the weather will keep them in their wickiups."

Charley lifted an eyebrow. "The Tonkawa is sly like the fox. He does that which you do not expect."

For several minutes after Matt disappeared into the forest, Charley One-Horse continued to look after his new friend. He raised his eyes heavenward and murmured a short prayer to Caddi Ayo, the Sky God.

Behind him came the soft crunch of feet on the snow. Joe muttered, "Where's Matt going?"

Keeping his eyes forward, Charley replied, "To do what he must."

The young boy came to stand beside the Caddo, his towhead coming to Charley's shoulder. "I don't understand."

"He be fine. Now come. This thing you call Christmas. We have much to do." With a faint smile, he looked down at Joe. "First, I show you and the small one to hunt and trap. Your children never go hungry."

Joe blushed. "I ain't going to have no children."

Charley laughed.

Instead of the winding trace, Matt remained in the forest where the snow lay not as thick, much of it blocked from the ground by the canopy of limbs and leaves on the spreading live oaks.

An hour from camp, he spotted movement behind the thick bole of a giant pine off to his left. He smiled when he made out the outline of a horse beside a fallen tree. The one that had bolted back at the owlhoots' camp.

When the horse spotted him he backed away, his eyes wide with fear, but the knot on the lead rope had wedged in the roots of a toppled oak.

Speaking softly, Matt approached the skittish pony and quickly fashioned a lark's head bridle by looping the rope around the pony's lower jaw. He swung onto the animal's back. The bay answered Matt's leads well, and the two of them made good time.

Three times before reaching the river, they crossed small streams. Matt paused to dig up some cattail roots to go with the flour cakes and venison he had packed in his parfleche bag.

Around noon, they hit the river and turned south, taking care to remain in the thick forest within sight of the turbulent and muddy Sabine River.

The wind picked up, sending a shiver down Matt's

spine. Suddenly, the bay's ears perked up, and the alert animal peered to the west. Ahead was a small clearing with thick understory clusters of wild azaleas. Matt reined the bay into the vegetation and dismounted, pinching the animal's nostrils to keep it from whinnying.

The bay continued staring to the west. Moments later, a band of Indians, mere shadows in the depths of the forest, rode slowly single file to the north. Looked like Charley had been right. The Tonkawas were on the move.

He waited for several minutes after the column vanished into the shadows before moving out.

"That's all we need, fella," he muttered to the bay, leaning forward and patting the animal's neck. "Killers ahead, and enemies behind. It sure don't make a hombre feel none too at home, do it?"

Just before dark, Matt caught the pungent aroma of woodsmoke. Coy's Landing. He rode a few minutes longer before searching for a suitable spot to spend the night. Down in a gully he discovered a thick tangle of mayhaw vines that would jerk a jasper from a sound sleep if anyone should try to squirm through them. After securing the bay and gathering an armful of graze for the animal, he set out for the landing.

Overhead, the clouds broke apart, pushed south by

the suddenly freshening north wind. Matt tugged his mackinaw tighter.

With a skeptical gleam in his eyes, Lester looked up at Charley. "Why don't we just shoot what we want to eat? That's what Pa and the others always did."

Both Mary Elizabeth and Joe Hill looked up at the Caddo, their eyes asking the same question.

"Too loud." Charley gestured to the two rifles leaning against the wall. "Save cartridges."

A sudden chill ran up Mary Elizabeth's spine. "Do you think Mr. Carson will come back?"

Charley shrugged. "Who can say? Out here, we alone. No help. The Great Spirit tells us to help ourselves. We pray to Him for help but make sure we not step on rattlesnake." He paused and smiled. "Come. I show you. Then we build throwing stick."

Joe and Lester exchanged puzzled looks. "A throwing stick?" Joe muttered.

"What's that?" Lester asked.

Charley grinned to himself. "Come. I show you."

The remainder of the morning, the Caddo warrior instructed the boys in various traps, beginning with the spring trap.

Over a well-traveled animal run, the Caddo showed the boys how to bend a supple tree and fasten it to an arresting trigger on another tree. From the arched trunk, he hung a noose over the trail. "Animal hits loop, tree goes up, jerks him off his feet."

Lester snorted. "What's to keep him from going around the noose?"

With an amused gleam in his eye, Charley held up one finger as if to say, "Watch." He quickly used his heavy knife to hew out a dozen wrist-sized limbs three feet long. Sharpening one end, he stuck them in the ground in a row parallel to the trail on either side. He stepped back. "Now, find small limbs and weave in sticks."

The frown on Lester's slender face turned into a knowing grin.

By noon, they had set half a dozen traps.

The remainder of the day they spent carving each young man a throwing stick, an implement of flattened wood with a groove eighteen inches long on one side. On one end was a handgrip and at the other, a cup.

Mary Elizabeth frowned. "I've never seen anything like that. What does it do?"

Remaining seated, Charley gripped the stick and raised it to his shoulder with the cup behind his back. "Make spears to fit stick." He made a throwing motion, pulling the stick forward as if he were hurling an imaginary spear. "Throw spears farther than with arm."

Lester's face lit in instant understanding. He grabbed the other throwing stick and made several practice throws. He grinned at his sister. "Jiminies, sis. Look at this."

Mary Elizabeth arched a skeptical eyebrow. "Just don't you two hurt each other."

Ignoring her admonition, Lester looked down at Charley. "When do we make the spears, huh? When?"

With a grunt, the Caddo rose from his soogan where he had been sitting cross-legged, and pulled back his blanket, retrieving two six-foot-long spears. The pointed ends were needle-sharp and fire-hardened.

Lester yelled with excitement and reached for one of the spears but Charley pulled them back. "Come morning is time enough."

"But, but, how does it work?" Lester's thin face was flush with excitement.

Charley took the throwing stick from Lester and rested it at his shoulder. He positioned the spear in the groove, butting the end into the cup. Without a word, he looked from Lester to Joe.

The boys nodded, and Joe said, "I see."

Chapter Eleven

Matt crouched behind a giant pine studying the square yellow lights punching holes in the darkness enveloping Coy's Landing. Laughter and shouts echoed from the sprawling building. Two small sloops at the dock rocked gently as the current of the Sabine tugged at them.

Several horses milled about the corral. Early in the evening, owners went out to check on their ponies, but as the darkness deepened the only occasional hombre ambling into the night was heading for the outhouse.

Easing forward in the shadows cast by the tall pines, Matt peered through the dingy windows into the saloon, searching for Carson and his band of cutthroats.

He spotted Carson in the rear of the saloon, seated at a table in front of a blazing fire with two of his gang. On the table at Carson's right arm lay a pair of saddlebags. Matt's eyes narrowed, wondering if the bag held his and Cotton's two thousand dollars in gold as well as the six thousand belonging to the wagon train.

Moments later, the last of the gang slid in at the table and reached for the whiskey. Matt grunted. He remembered them all—Horrells, Carson, Higgins, and Dow, cowards each and every one and deathly afraid of Ed Carson. That had been obvious on the journey from Westport Landing.

He grinned when he spotted the knot on Higgins' forehead above two black eyes and the bandages around Dow's head. That bear must have caused a heap of excitement back in camp.

Around the room, a dozen or so more hombres sat at tables or slumped over the bar, their fingers clutching tumblers of whiskey or mugs of beer. The night was raw, and the whiskey warmed the belly.

From the gesturing around the table, Matt guessed the owlhoots were discussing the split of the gold.

Pink Higgins chugged his whiskey and poured another, looking for enough to stiffen his backbone. "Sure, I know you figure someone is still alive, Ed, but I just want what's coming to me." He glanced around the table. "All of us do. I say we split it up and then every man for hisself. Me, I'm going down to Mexico."

While Carson's attention was on Higgins, Wes Horrells slid a furtive hand under the table and slipped his six-gun onto his lap just in case Carson tried to back out of their deal. With only four of them left, his take was two thousand dollars. He'd have to work five or six years for that kind of money.

Carson eyed Higgins coldly then glanced at Blacky Dow. "What about you, Blacky?"

While Dow was just as greedy as the others, he was some smarter. He'd wait until he caught Carson off guard. "Whatever you got in mind, Ed, is fine with me."

His eyes cold, Carson cut them to Horrells. "Wes?"

The smaller man lost his nerve. He gulped, shot a furtive glance at Higgins then nodded briefly. "Whatever you say, Ed."

Carson studied the faces looking at him. Maybe they were right. Maybe his best move was to split the loot and head for the high lonesome where a soul could lose himself from searching eyes forever. Of course, he reminded himself, he'd be a heap better off if he didn't have to split the loot.

He downed his whiskey. "Tell you what, boys. I got the gold in a safe place where I can get to it right easy. It's getting late. We'll divvy up in the morning and go our separate ways." He paused and eyed them narrowly, the threat in his black eyes obvious. "Unless you think I might try to run out on you tonight." His tone dared them to agree with him.

Horrells gulped. He shook his head. "Not me, Ed. Morning's fine with me."

"Yeah. Me too," Higgins said. He hesitated, his eyes on the saddlebags. "You sure it's in a safe place?"

Carson's jaw grew hard. "I said so, didn't I?"

Nodding vigorously, Higgins blurted out, "Yeah. Yeah. You sure did, Ed."

As one light after another flickered out in the saloon and hotel, Matt eased into the barn at one end of the corral, finding a spot out of the bitter wind where he could keep an eye on the hotel. If Ed Carson left, he wanted to see him.

Matt jerked awake when one of the ponies snickered. He squinted into the shadows cast by the starlight. A figure was easing toward the corral. When he reached the corral rails, the shadow paused to glance back at the dark building.

The reflecting light from the snow lit Carson's grizzled face. Unable to believe his luck, Matt slipped from his bed in the straw and crouched in the shadows cast by the wall of the barn as the large silhouette ducked through the rails and glided across the corral. Matt's fingers closed around one end of a singletree.

Just as Carson reached the barn, he froze, his head

cocked so that Matt knew the jasper was staring into the inky blackness of the barn. The only sounds beyond the steady whistle of the north wind were the snuffling of a few ponies and the sucking and popping sounds of their hooves in the mud. After several long seconds, the figure took an object from his shoulder and draped it over the top rail of the stall.

Matt's pulse raced. The gold.

Carson moved quickly to his horse. His hands flew as he slipped on the bridle. He grabbed his saddle, and when he turned his back to throw the saddle on his pony, Matt rose silently from the shadows.

Carson heard the jingle of metal against metal.

Then his head exploded.

Matt stood over the fallen outlaw. He was still alive, so the lanky cowpoke dragged him from under the horses' hooves, leaving the unconscious hardcase slumped against the wall of the barn.

Twenty minutes later, Matt, astride the bay, was heading back to the cave, taking his time and picking his way through the forest. Back at the landing, he had tried to mix his tracks with the others, but he knew if the outlaws cast about far enough, they'd find a single set coming out of the forest, and a single set returning.

He glanced down at the saddlebags in front of him. The reassuring weight when they bounced against the inside of his thighs made him grin.

The grin faded when he remembered the column of Indians he had spotted the day before. He had to take care not to run upon their camp.

As the sun rose, a gust of wind sweeping down the gully rattled the heavy bearskin and wood-latticed door. Charley grunted and pushed to his feet. “We run traps.”

Joe reached for his coat and hat. “I’m ready.”

Lester whined, “I don’t want to go. It’s too cold out there.”

Surprised, Mary Elizabeth looked out from behind the canvas in front of her soogan at her brother. The young boy never turned down the chance to get out of the cave. She took a step toward him. “Don’t you feel all right, Lester?”

He glanced at the floor. “Yes, but I just don’t feel like going outside right now.”

She reached out to lay her hand on his forehead but he shoved it away. “I said I feel all right.” He glared at her defiantly. “I just don’t want to go outside.”

Charley shrugged at Joe. “Come. We go.”

No sooner had the canvas and bearskin door fallen back in place, the young boy leaped to his feet and grabbed a throwing stick. Hastily, he dug a spear from under Charley’s soogan and despite Mary Elizabeth’s protestations, fit it in the throwing stick.

He bounced around the tree like a little Indian, pretending to throw the spear. "Look at me, Mary Elizabeth. Look!"

She stamped her foot. "Put it up, Lester. Do you hear me? I said put it up." She turned and disappeared behind the canvas.

He snorted. "I ain't hurting nothing."

"I said, put it up."

The two siblings argued for several minutes. Mary Elizabeth clenched her teeth. "You put it up, or I'll have Matt take it away from you." She turned on her heel and stormed behind the drape separating her pallet from the remainder of the cave.

The young boy glared at the canvas. "I ain't going to—"

At that moment, the door jerked open and a war-painted Indian stepped inside, momentarily surprised by the scene before him.

For several moments, the startled Indian stared at Lester. Without warning, he bared his lips in a snarl.

Mary Elizabeth stepped into the room from behind the canvas drape and screamed. The Indian spun on her, raising his war club.

At that moment, Lester hurled the spear, and the sharp missile caught the savage in the side, just below the ribs. A scream burst from the savage's lips, and he dropped the war club, seizing the spear in both hands and tugging it from his side.

Mary Elizabeth grabbed the pot of boiling water

from the fire and threw it on the savage. He screamed even louder and burst from the cave. Scrambling up the side of the gully, he disappeared into the forest.

Moments later, Charley and Joe rushed in. Joe's face was red with alarm. "Who was that Indian running away from here?"

Hastily, Mary Elizabeth, her cheeks flushed with excitement and fear, told them what had taken place. Immediately, Charley ordered the three to stay put and on guard, then set out on the trail of the wounded Indian.

Thirty minutes later, Charley returned, telling them only that the Indian, a Tonkawa, would be of no further danger to them. "But, no fire, no smoke."

Later, the clouds returned, and the snow began to fall. Mid-afternoon, Matt, having left the bay back down the trail, trudged in, his saddlebags over his shoulder and a frown on his face. "What is wrong?" He glanced around the cave. "No fire."

Charley gestured to the west. "Tonkawa. One come early this morning. I kill. They will search for him when he no return."

Scratching the week-old beard on his jaw, Matt glanced out the cave. "It's snowing again. Will it continue?"

The Caddo grunted. "All night."

"Then maybe we can have us a small fire."

"If you say."

Matt handed him the saddlebags. "You know the hollow tree down by the creek?"

"Yes."

"Hide this there. I will be back. I have a plan."

Thirty minutes later, he swung onto the back of the bay and cut through the forest to the massacre clearing. From there he headed back down the road toward the river, not bothering to cover his tracks. As he passed under a limb hanging over the narrow road, he swung off and clambered to the ground on the far side of the tree.

The bay paused, looked back, then continued.

"You think that will fool the Indians?" Joe frowned up at Matt from where the young boy sat cross-legged in front of the tiny fire.

Matt tugged off his snow-soaked boots. "Hard to say. They'll look for their scout. When they can't find him, they'll be suspicious. If we're lucky, the tracks of the bay are the only tracks they'll find."

Lester's stomach growled, and he pulled his coat tighter about his narrow shoulders. "I'm hungry." He nodded to the fire. "Can't we build this up?"

Mary Elizabeth skewered a slab of cold venison on a slender stick and handed it to her brother. "Here. Hold this over the fire."

Charley spoke up, referring to the column of riders Matt had spotted in the forest a day earlier. “How many you see?”

“Can’t say exactly. They was a long piece off and all blurred together. I’d guess twelve, thirteen.”

Silently, he rose to his feet. “You stay, you sleep. I will watch.”

Chapter Twelve

An hour after Matt cold-cocked Ed Carson, rough hands jerked the big man awake. Blinking against the daylight, he grunted and shook his head in an effort to disperse the cobwebs tangling his thoughts.

Gruff voices cut through the fuzziness in his head.

"Ed. Wake up. What happened?"

Pink Higgins growled suspiciously, "What are you doing out here?" He glanced at Blacky Dow, who eyed him knowingly. Carson's pony had a saddle blanket on its back, and the saddle lay in the mud at the horse's feet. Both owlhoots knew exactly what Carson was doing out in the barn. He was planning on running off with their share of the gold. Behind Higgins, Wes Horrells looked around for the saddlebags.

Groaning, Carson rubbed the back of his neck and

struggled to his feet. When his eyes finally focused, he saw his three compadres eyeing him suspiciously.

"Where's the gold?" Horrells demanded.

Dow's eyes narrowed. "Yeah. You weren't thinking about running out on us, were you, Ed?"

"Huh? What the Sam Hill are you—" Suddenly, he remembered—the clink of metal, the numbing blow to his head. Shoving the three aside, he strode forward. "The saddlebags. Where are the saddlebags? Look for them."

Higgins muttered in stunned disbelief. "Our gold? You lost it?"

Carson turned on him like a savage lobo wolf. "I didn't lose it, you idiot! Somebody stole it. That's what happened." He glared at them, his blazing black eyes daring them to dispute him.

His brain raced. A rugged and uneducated hombre who made his living from the underbelly of society, Carson possessed the animal instinct for survival. He thought fast and acted even faster. In the animal kingdom, the stronger, the more aggressive prevail. It was the same at his level of life. "I came out a few minutes ago to saddle up. I told you we were leaving early after we made the split. I had the saddlebags with me—for safekeeping." He looked around the barn and spotted the singletree in the mud. "Whoever the jasper was, that's what he used."

Dow and Higgins exchanged skeptical looks but neither owlhoot spoke his mind.

Carson studied them for a moment, seeing the cynicism in their eyes. He dropped his large hand to the butt of his Colt. "Well, do you believe me?" His tone implied that if they figured he was lying then they best slap leather.

Horrells swallowed his suspicions. "I believe you, Ed. I sure do. That was a lowdown trick, sneaking up on you and cold-cocking you like that."

Dow nodded briefly. "Sure, Ed. Whatever you say."

Higgins nodded to the sprawling inn from which smoke was drifting from the stovepipes. "Who do you reckon stole our money? Someone in there?"

Carson spat in the mud at his feet. "No one in there knew about it unless"—he paused to fix them with a piercing look—"unless one of you talked too much."

As one, the three shook their heads.

"Not me," Higgins muttered.

Carson studied the barn, then slid his gaze through the corral rails to the forest beyond.

Dow cleared his throat. "Maybe whoever did it didn't know what was in them saddlebags. Maybe he was just looking for a few greenbacks or something to sell."

Higgins and Horrells looked up at Carson hopefully.

The big man nodded, his eyes remaining fixed on the forest beyond. "Could be." He paused, pursed his lips, and narrowed his eyes. "But, I don't think so. Why just the saddlebags?"

Horrells frowned. "Huh?"

The more Carson considered the situation, the more convinced he became that whoever had jumped him and taken the saddlebags was not from Coy's Landing. He shook his head. "Why didn't he take my horse and gear? No. He was after the gold. He knew where it was. I was right. We did miss someone at the wagon train. I don't know who the rogue is, but he's the hombre what jumped me."

Dow wanted to sneer but he feared Carson's knotted fists. "You can't be certain, Ed. What if it is someone here, and they get away. We'll never find them."

A faint sneer split Carson's bearded face. "If I'm right, that one left his horse in the forest. I wouldn't be surprised if we don't find his sign out there."

The three owlhoots looked at each other wearily.

Fifteen minutes later, a hundred yards from the landing, Carson called them over and pointed out a set of tracks leading back into the pine and oak forest. The big man squatted and touched the tip of a dirt-encrusted fingernail to one of the tracks. "Fresh. Not over a couple hours old." He looked up into the steady north breeze. "Wind ain't had a chance to knock off the edges."

Shucking his six-gun, he rose and followed the sign to where Matt had tied the bay in the patch of mayhaw vines. A pile of horse biscuits indicated the pony had been there several hours. A smug grin curled Carson's lips when he saw the direction the tracks had taken. "That's what I thought," he muttered, more to himself than the others. "That no-account is heading directly back to the wagon train. Someone did make it out alive, and he's the one what stole my gold."

Dow narrowed his eyes when he heard Carson's last remark. He started to correct his boss that the gold was theirs, not just his, but he kept silent, unspoken resolve reminding him not to turn his back on the big man when they did retrieve the gold.

"All right," Carson growled. "Let's saddle up. We'll take a packhorse with enough gear to stay a few days."

Several times Carson lost the trail. He grunted in admiration at the jasper's trail smarts, but even when he lost the sign, he kept moving northwest, knowing eventually he would cross the road that would lead him back to the site of the massacre.

Mid-afternoon, Carson muttered a curse when new snow began falling. He wasn't worried about losing the trail but that they might be facing another bad storm. He glanced over his shoulder at the packhorse loaded with shelter and food and grinned. They had nothing to worry about.

"Blast," he growled, fishing a pint of Old Crow whiskey from the pocket of his Yankee greatcoat. "Ain't never seen weather like this in years."

Behind him, Higgins hissed. “Ed. Over yonder to the east, near the river. Something’s moving.”

As one, the four reined up behind a tangle of mayhaw vines. Far into the distance, the oak and pine trunks faded into shadows, within the shadows came indistinct movement.

Horrells muttered, “What do you think, Ed?”

“Shut up,” the big man growled.

His horse’s ears perked forward.

The movement drew closer.

Higgins chuckled. “It’s just a horse. Let’s go.”

Carson threw up his arm. “Hold on.” He muttered a curse. “Blasted Injuns.”

“Injuns? Where?”

“You blind? Following back behind the horse.” He drew a deep breath. “Don’t move. They can’t see us.”

As the outlaws watched, three warriors picked up the single pony and headed back in the direction from which they had come.

Long after the Indians disappeared, the four men sat staring after them. Finally, Horrells spoke up. “Now what? I ain’t crazy about riding into a heap of Injuns.”

Carson sneered. “Even for your share of eight thousand dollars?”

“Won’t do me no good if my scalp’s hanging in some buck’s lodge.”

The big man looked at his other two compadres. "You feel the same way?"

Higgins drew a deep breath and stared at the ground at his pony's feet. Dow cleared his throat. "Not exactly, but I reckon I wouldn't mind knowing what them Injuns is up to. For all we know, they might just be passing through. After all, we never saw no sign of them when we was up here last time."

Carson looked around the forest. "We got grub and a tent. I say we stay here for the night. In the morning, I'll ride out and see what I can see."

Dow studied the larger man. "Sounds sensible. I'll ride with you."

Carson eyed him shrewdly, a faint grin on his lips.

Finally, the snowy gray afternoon turned into night, and with the setting of the sun behind the clouds, the night grew even colder. Outside the tent, the wind howled.

Charley One-Horse ducked into the cave, brushing the snow from his shoulders and stomping it from his beaded moccasins. He tossed Matt a pair of knee-length deerskin moccasins.

The lean cowpoke arched an eyebrow.

Charley shrugged and without a trace of a smile, said, "A Tonk lost them." With a nod of assurance, he placed two or three branches on the fire to build it up, then took a cup of steaming cassina tea offered him by Mary Elizabeth and squatted by the fire. "It went as you hoped," he said, relating the events of the afternoon. "The Tonks follow the bay horse. They return to their camp near the river of clear water back to the sun. They burn many fires." He nodded to the small one before them. "Ours they will not smell."

"The camp, is it a long one?"

Charley shrugged. "I know more come the sun, but I think no more than one night."

"Where do they go?"

"I think maybe to the Wichita or my people. They wear war paint." He frowned. "Whatever is to happen, I think it is not good."

"What about the missing warrior?"

The somber Caddo made a sweeping gesture that took in the whole forest. "He like grain of sand on the shore of the great river. Not find. If he alive, he will return."

Chapter Thirteen

With the graying of dawn, Charley One-Horse slipped through the snow-covered forest to the Tonkawa camp. Matt and Joe headed in the other direction, planning on running the snares along the meandering creek.

At the same time several miles southeast, Ed Carson and Blacky Dow rode out of their camp, planning on striking the winding road leading to the scene of the massacre.

Joe had taken his spear thrower and spear, practicing throwing as they trudged through the calf-deep snow. The young boy glanced at Matt's moccasins. "Don't the snow soak through them none?"

"They waterproof them."

"How do they go about that?"

Matt pulled up at the first snare from which dangled a fat rabbit. He removed the rabbit and tied it to his belt. "Every tribe has a different method. Most of them smoke the skins. They—" Without warning, he froze and whispered. "Don't move."

"Huh?"

"Quiet. You have your spear thrower ready?"

"Yes, but—"

"Don't move a muscle. Not yet. Just your eyes. Over to your right. About thirty feet. A rabbit—on a log. Here's a chance to see what you can do."

The young boy caught his breath.

"Wait until he looks away, then move, but move slow."

When Joe spotted the rabbit, his heart jumped into his throat and his pulse raced. As he slowly lifted the spear thrower, he felt the muscles in his arm begin to tremble. He flexed his thin fingers about the handgrip.

"Steady," Matt whispered. "Take your time."

Joe gulped hard. He could feel his whole body shaking. The twenty seconds it took him to ready his throw seemed like two hours.

"Now?" he whispered to Matt.

"Whenever you're ready, boy."

In the next instant, Joe hurled the spear. The whooshing sound of the spear thrower breaking the still air alerted the rabbit. The long shaft whistled just over the rabbit's head.

The startled ball of fur darted into the forest.

"Dad gum. I missed him. Dad gum, dad gum, dad gum."

Matt clapped him on the shoulder. "Maybe so, but not by much. Now get your spear and load up again. Might see something else down here."

The next two snares held rabbits but the last three only the remains. Matt quickly tossed the bloody fur away and reset the snares, knowing that whatever creature had eaten the rabbits would return. It had found three easy meals, and whatever it was it would not forget.

Joe examined the partially eaten bodies. "What do you figure ate them?"

"Look." Matt pointed to the pugmarks in the snow. "See the four-clawed toes and the heel that looks like a triangle?"

"What made them?"

"Could be fox or coyote. From the size, I'd guess coyote. Come on. Let's see where our little bandit is going." Matt followed the trail of the hungry little thief.

The trail paralleled the meandering creek. After a mile or so, Joe gasped, "Look at that." He pointed across the creek to a steep bluff, its face covered with a thick layer of vines.

Matt studied the bluff warily. It was over a quarter

of a mile long and at least a hundred feet high. The coyote tracks led directly to the face of the bluff and disappeared into a small cave.

Moving slowly along the creek, Matt studied the tangle of vines, noting several caves along the way, some large enough to provide his small party shelter or refuge in an emergency.

"Wait here," he told the young boy as he waded through the creek for a closer look at the bluff. Several feet up, he spotted a large opening. Quickly, he climbed the vines and peered over the rim of the cave's mouth. The cave smelled of dried dust.

He nodded to himself. Later, he would return with a torch and explore the cave.

Charley One-Horse studied the Tonkawa camp from the fork of an ancient red oak. The Tonks had thrown up temporary lean-tos of deerskin and bear hide, indicating to the Caddo that they were in no hurry to move on.

He frowned. *Why would a war party hesitate so?* He pondered the question a few moments until the answer hit him between the eyes. They were waiting for others. He grimaced. If that were so, it was bad news, worse than he had first believed.

Mid-afternoon, another dozen Tonkawas rode in. Charley eyed them without emotion. He had been right. Now what would they do?

* * *

Earlier, Ed Carson and Blacky Dow had pulled up at noon in a tangle of vines near the trace. Movement in the thick forest to the southwest had caught their attention.

Carson's eyes narrowed at he counted twelve warriors heading north.

At his side, Dow muttered, "You reckon they're joining up with them we saw last night?"

"Hard to say. I don't know what tribe they are. For all we know, they might be planning on jumping that other bunch."

"Maybe, and maybe not."

Carson chuckled. "After they ride on, we'll ease a little farther along. Find us a place to fort up and see what happens."

Thirty minutes later, Carson clicked his tongue and urged his pony forward. "Now, let's us see what we can see."

The two owlhoots remained back in the forest, leaving the snow in the road untouched, unmarked.

A few minutes later, Dow pointed to torn-up snow ahead. "That's where they passed." The trail led to the trace then cut northwest. "We follow it, or what?"

Carson grunted. "Up to the road." He studied the forest about them. "Unless I miss my guess, we ought to be close to the wagon train."

When they reached the trace, Carson reined up. He studied the winding road to his left and back to his right in the direction of the river. This part of the forest was unfamiliar to him.

"Which way now?" Dow scratched his bearded jaw.

"Back that way," Carson replied, heading back toward the river and familiar territory.

Ten minutes later, they spotted the massacre site. "There it is," Carson gloated. He shot a glance over his shoulders. "I don't know where them Injuns went but they're back behind us a piece."

Dow grinned with relief and pulled out his bag of Bull Durham. "That's good." He started building a cigarette.

Carson growled. "What are you trying to do? Bring every Injun within ten miles running after us?"

"Huh?"

"Them Injuns got noses sharp as starving wolves. You light that cigarette, and every one of them heathens will smell it."

Chagrinned, Dow tossed the cigarette on the snow. "So, what do we do now?"

The big man studied the forest. "We look. You ride east. I'll head north. Ride ten minutes, then come back. If we don't spot something, we'll ride out a little farther."

Dow nodded. He cut his eyes over his shoulder in the direction the warriors had taken and shivered. He flipped the loop off the hammer of his six-gun.

* * *

Charley waited an hour after the last party of Tonks rode in before he was satisfied that the warriors would spend at least one more night before moving out.

Easing to the snow-covered ground, he made his way back through the forest. He crept along beside a deadfall. Suddenly, he froze, his black eyes focused on two cowpokes bundled against the cold a short distance ahead.

Slipping behind a ball of bare roots, the Caddo warrior recognized the two as the owlhoots he and Matt had spied upon a few days earlier. They were of the band that had savagely murdered all on the wagon train except for those back in the cave.

Charley watched as one headed north, another east. He nodded slowly when he realized they were searching for Matt and the others. When the two were out of sight, he hurried to the spot from which they had departed, then raced west along the winding trace, making sure his tracks were clear and sharp so the owlhoots would have no trouble following them.

A light snow began to fall.

Charley muttered a curse, hoping it was not so heavy as to cover his tracks.

When he caught the odor of woodsmoke, he knew he had followed the trace as far as he dared. He leaped over a stretch of unmarked snow and landed behind an ancient white oak, which he climbed high into the crown and found himself a snug little nest in the fork of four great branches.

And waited anxiously.

Five minutes later, he heard the faint click of O-rings.

Back to the east, Carson and Dow rode toward him, their eyes fixed apprehensively on a set of single tracks on the trace.

Quickly, the Caddo shucked his six-gun, crouched deep into the fork, and fired a shot into the air.

Below, Carson and Dow reined up. The two grizzled killers exchanged fearful looks.

Ahead of them, several faint "Yip, yip, yips" echoed through the forest. The two owlhoots jerked their horses around and raced for the river.

As they rounded a bend in the trace, Dow glanced to his left into the forest and caught a fleeting glance of a young boy. He blinked and looked again but the boy had vanished.

The shrill war cries behind him made him forget everything else but his own safety.

Half a dozen Tonkawas pursued the two owlhoots for several minutes before turning back. They had no reason to look over their shoulder but even if they had, chances were slim they would have spotted the laughing face of Charley One-Horse high in the white oak.

* * *

When Pink Higgins and Wes Horrells heard the distant pop of gunfire, they hastily grabbed their saddle guns and took refuge behind a snow-covered deadfall.

After a few moments, the firing ceased, but the two waddies kept their eyes on the dark forest about them.

An hour passed. They heard nothing, saw nothing.

Horrells dragged the tip of his tongue over his dry lips. "What do you think?"

Higgins kept his eyes moving, searching the thick woods. "Got no idea. Me, I'm all for heading back to the landing." He shook his head. "I don't feel none too comfortable just the two of us out here all by our lonesomes."

Chapter Fourteen

Charley had slipped within hearing of the Tonks before they rose next morning. He watched from inside a hollow log as they rode out, heading west on the trace. While he knew only bits and pieces of the Tonk language, he smiled to himself when he heard the word "Wichitas" bandied about. And when a Tonk warrior pointed northwest, Charley knew his own people were not in danger.

"You're certain of that, huh?" Matt sipped his cassina tea.

Charley gave a terse nod. "Yes. They leave forest."

"Good. With Carson heading back to the river, we're safe for the time being."

The boys cheered with glee. A smile wreathed

Mary Elizabeth's face. Matt added with a grin, "I reckon that means that there's nothing standing in the way of a nice Christmas for us, huh?"

The boys shouted their agreement.

Mary Elizabeth cleared her throat. "Did you know some people have turkey at Christmas?"

Charley and Matt exchanged puzzled looks. The last few years during the war, if Matt celebrated Christmas, it was with whatever he could forage from the countryside.

She saw the confused looks on their faces. "I don't mean for us to have it, but I know they're around because I've heard them gobbling. I just thought that—"

"Well, hold on now," Matt said. He looked at the boys. "These young men are learning to use their spears, and they're not bad at setting snares. What do you think, boys? How would you like turkey and venison for Christmas?"

If any Tonkawas had been within a mile of the tree, they would have heard the boys' shouts of approval.

Mary Elizabeth eyed the gleeful boys. She cut her eyes to Matt and Charley, then quickly looked away. She had an idea of her own.

The next day, Charley and the boys set out to run the traps and locate a turkey roost. Matt and Mary headed for the creek to dig cattail potatoes and break dried berry vines to add extra flavor to the cassina tea.

To the boys' disappointment, the preying coyote had eaten four of the rabbits, and while they spotted several turkeys, they could never approach close enough to take a shot at them with the spear thrower.

Instead, they followed the sign to a roost—several towering maples. Sign on the new snow made it evident that the roost was a large one.

"Tomorrow, we build trap," Charley announced that night. "Catch many turkey."

The next morning, not far from the turkey roost, Charley and Lester built a tunnel several feet long and three feet high of sticks woven together and knotted with strips of canvas. They blocked one end and fashioned a gate that swung down at the other. To the gate, they fastened strips of canvas that they would use to lower the gate.

Using the seed corn they had salvaged from the wagon train, they laid a trail from the roost through the open mouth of the trap all the way to the end.

"Now, we wait," the Caddo whispered, ducking behind the snow-covered root ball of an ancient oak.

Lester, his face flushed with excitement, whispered, "When will they come?"

"When they come. Now listen. Say nothing."

Half a dozen times in the next hour, Lester asked the same question, and Charley gave him the same answer, "When they come."

* * *

At the same time, Matt and Joe crouched behind a tangle of understory vegetation, watching a small pond formed by the narrow creek. The snow around the edge of the pond was torn by animal tracks, among them several deer.

"Sure hope we see one," Joe muttered. He hefted his spear thrower. "I've been practicing, and a deer is a lot bigger than a rabbit."

"And a lot spookier," Matt reminded him.

At Coy's Landing, Ed Carson sat around a battered table dealing out hands of poker and drinking bad whiskey. "A boy, you say? You saw a boy back there in the woods?"

Blacky Dow retrieved his dealt card. "Yep. Just caught a glimpse of him. But I saw one."

Pink Higgins frowned. "No boy cold-cocked you out in the barn, Ed. That means there's got to be at least two of them out there somewheres."

"Yeah." Wes Horrells nodded and tossed down his drink.

Carson dealt the last card to each of them. "That's what I figure." He glanced out the window at the light flakes of falling snow.

Dow studied his cards then bet a dollar. "We're going back, ain't we?"

Flexing his thick fingers, Carson picked up five dollars. "Call and raise you four. And to answer your question, you bet, but not in this snow. I ain't all that familiar with this part of the country, but from what I hear this is unusual weather. Some of the old boys around here ain't never seen this much snow in the last thirty years. First day of sunshine, we're heading out. And this time we ain't coming back without the eight thousand."

Two or three times, Lester looked at Charley and rolled his eyes as if to say they quit for the day. Each time, the Caddo shook his head.

And now, mid-afternoon, the wait was paying off.

Lester froze and stared up at Charley when he heard the first faint gobbling deep in the shadows of the forest.

Charley held a finger to his lips.

The gobbling deep in the shadows grew closer until, finally, Lester spotted one, then two, then three more, all following the trail of seed corn.

Charley laid his hand on Lester's shoulder and gently pressed him lower behind the tangle of vines behind which they crouched.

The Caddo warrior had cautioned Lester about the spookiness of turkeys. "They hear a noise, they stare at it for heap long time. No noise."

Lester quickly saw Charley's warning was accurate, for the turkeys moved slowly, pausing every few steps to survey the forest before continuing to feed.

After what seemed like hours, three turkeys entered the trap, working their way to the end.

Lester looked up at Charley expectantly. The Caddo smiled to himself at the excitement in the boy's eyes. Tersely, he nodded, and Lester yanked on the trapline.

With a dull thud, the gate slammed shut.

In the next instant, the frightened turkeys began squawking.

Lester raced to the trap, throwing his weight against the gate to keep the turkeys from escaping. Cheeks flushed, his breath coming in gasps, he grinned up at Charley. "Now what?"

Charley grinned. "Open gate. Grab one."

But when Lester opened the gate, the turkeys retreated to the rear of the trap. He frowned up at the grinning Caddo. "What do I do now?"

Charley gestured to the interior of the trap. "Crawl in. Grab by feet."

Lester stared at him. He looked around at the tunnel trap. "In there?"

"Keep hat on and head down."

Taking a deep breath, Lester straightened his shoulders and crawled inside. The squawking and gobbling was ear-splitting but the young boy made his way a few feet down the tunnel. Without a warning, a young tom fluffed up and charged him. Remembering Charley's advice, Lester ducked his head and grabbed at the turkey when the squawking bird hit.

He grabbed the turkey by both feet and backed out, dragging the frantic bird with him. Outside, Charley quickly wrung the turkey's neck then looked at Lester, who was grinning from ear to ear despite a few scratches on his face.

With a glint of amusement in his dark eyes, Charley said, "You want another?"

The young boy eyed the trap and the two remaining birds warily. He wasn't any too anxious to crawl back in there. He nodded firmly. "I think one'll be enough for us, don't you?"

With a chuckle, Charley nodded to the others. "Turn loose. Leave seed. They come back."

While Matt and Joe spotted a few deer, none came within range of either the spear thrower or the bois d'arc bow. "We'll try again tomorrow," Matt said.

Overhead, squirrels chattered, then darted into their nests or holes. "Wish we could get us a batch of squirrel," Joe muttered, staring darkly up at the nimble creatures bouncing around on the limbs and laughing at them.

Matt grunted and held up the bow. "Maybe Charley could, but I'm not that much of a shot with arrows." Then an idea hit. "Still, I got me a notion of how we might use those little critters come Christmas dinner."

Joe frowned. "How's that?"

Matt had a sly grin. "I'll tell you later. Right now, just mark all the squirrel nests you see."

Chapter Fifteen

After Matt and Joe stomped the snow off their feet by the fire, the rawhide-tough cowpoke realized there would be no need for extra venison for Christmas dinner. The haunches they had would be sufficient.

Not only had Lester and Charley brought in a nice tom turkey for roasting, Mary Elizabeth had trapped a dozen fat crappie, bass, and perch.

"I didn't plan on being left out," she explained. "Everyone else was bringing in something for dinner. I reckoned I would too."

They laughed, and as they did, a gust of north wind howled down the gully. Charley glanced at Matt. "More snow."

Joe laughed. "Let it snow. We got all we need here."

He paused and looked at Matt. "How long to Christmas?"

Matt shrugged and surveyed the faces looking up at him. "I don't know. How does two days sound?"

The shout of laughter was his answer.

Snow filled the air the following day. Matt and Charley disappeared that morning only to return before noon, having spotted nothing of which they needed to be concerned.

Mid-afternoon, Matt and Joe headed out into the forest. "You remember where all the squirrel nests are?"

Joe shrugged. "Yeah. Why?"

"Because we're going to rob them."

Two hours later, they returned to the cave with a bag bulging with acorns, pecans, and hickory nuts. After shucking the hulls, they found over half of the nuts were good, offering a tasty stuffing for the turkey on the coming day.

Mary Elizabeth had returned to the creek, digging a pot of cattail roots and removing a large slab of the second skin of a box elder maple to sweeten the boiled potatoes.

While she mixed up fried corn cakes sweetened with the juice of maple, Matt stirred up a batch of cassina tea with an abundance of dried blackberry vines.

* * *

Christmas day dawned in the midst of a raging blizzard.

Inside the cave, a cozy fire licked at the golden-brown turkey turning on the spit. In a pot on the edge of the coals, the sweet aroma of boiling potatoes mixed with the mouthwatering bouquet of broiling venison and grilling turkey stuffed with a succulent mixture of hickories and pecans. On another edge of the fire sizzled fry cakes of corn and flour rolled in honey.

In another pot, cassina tea boiled, its sweet-smelling tendrils drifting into the air.

They sat around the fire, cross-legged, recounting Christmas memories. Charley grinned at Matt, who cleared his throat. "I don't know much about Christmas but I do know it is the time for gifts."

Mary Elizabeth frowned.

Before she could reply, Matt continued, "Now, stuck out here like we are, gifts are hard to come by, but me and Charley put something together we think you'll like." He nodded to Charley, who dug under his soogan and came up with two new spears for the boys' spear throwers.

"Now you have second spear if you miss the first," he announced, grinning down at the boys.

"And we didn't forget you, Miss Mary," Matt said, fishing a skin-covered object from beneath his own soogan. "It isn't the fanciest around but it'll work."

Surprised, she opened the gift. Her eyes widened, then tears gathered in them as she looked upon a hand-carved wooden comb. A wave of emotion flooded over her, and she pressed the gift to her bosom. "This—this is the best Christmas present I ever had," she said to Matt. "Thank you."

Matt's ears burned. "Thank Charley too. He's the one that found the hickory wood. He claims that it'll last forever."

Choking out her words, she thanked Charley, all the while her teary eyes fixed on the blushing face of the lean cowpoke across the fire.

Lester piped up. "I don't know about everyone else, but I'm hungrier than a wolf."

By the time the fire burned low, every bone on the turkey was bare, the venison devoured, fish bones picked clean, the boiled potatoes gone, the fry cakes gobbled down, and the pot of cassina tea was empty.

That night as Matt drifted off to sleep with the howling of the storm outside and the warmth of the fire and friends inside, he couldn't remember when he had enjoyed a day so.

The sun rose the next morning in a brittle blue sky.

Standing on the rim of the gully, Charley studied the sky. "Good weather. No snow." He held up his hands to indicate his uncertainty, then gestured to a point in the sky. "When the moon is there. No more."

Matt figured the Caddo was talking about at least one week of good weather. That would be more than enough time to move out of the area. Wherever Ed Carson was, he knew of their presence. Matt couldn't take the chance on the killer returning while they remained. He gestured to the southwest. "It's about time we make our move then. We'll head that way. Today."

Charley nodded. "I go with you."

Matt slid his hat to the back of his head. "Why?" He glanced to the northeast. "Your people are there. Do you not wish to go to them?"

"You save Charley's life. It is yours."

Matt studied him a moment, then held out his hand. "Friends."

Charley grinned. "Friends."

Matt scratched at his bearded jaw. He needed to shave soon but that could wait. Now they needed food for their journey.

He touched his finger to his chest. "I'll find us venison. You make all ready to leave."

Taking the Yellowboy Henry, Matt disappeared into the woods. Carson's gang had left the forest; the Tonkawas had moved on; so there was no one around to hear the single report from a rifle. It was still a risk, and Matt recognized it, but they had to move fast.

He glanced at the clear sky above them. They had no time to waste.

Moving silently, Matt moved like a shadow through the forest until he cut the sign of deer, a doe according to the imprints in the snow. He moved even slower, delicately tracking the small animal.

Her trail meandered through the forest, crossing the creek, then ascending the back of the sheer bluff Matt had discovered earlier.

The morning air was crisp and frigid. The crystal chirping of snowbirds echoed through the trees. His eyes ever moving, Matt eased up the back of the bluff, taking his time, studying the rising slopes above him.

Her tracks indicated that so far, he had not startled her. He continued tracking, remembering the lessons taught him in his youth.

How many times had he lain motionless in the sand behind purple sage, or on blistering rocks for his prey? Today, this task was even more important for the lives of three lay in his hands. The Caddo, a wily warrior, could take care of himself, but the young woman and the two boys—he shook his head. Without him, they would never survive the winter.

Stealthily, he crept upward, taking refuge behind the bare limbs of shrubs and vines.

Then he spotted the doe, browsing a few feet below the crest of the slope. Before he could ease the butt of the Henry to his shoulder, she darted forward, startled.

Matt frowned. What frightened her? Not he. He had been motionless, and he was downwind. She could not have picked up his scent. He crouched lower, peering over each shoulder at the slope below but seeing nothing.

After a few moments, still puzzled, he slipped forward, once again spotting the doe browsing on some wild azalea leaves. And once again, before he could fit his rifle to his shoulder, she moved.

Matt froze. The silence surrounding him echoed in his ears. It seemed he could hear her nibbling. Finally, he took a step, then another. Perhaps it was the upward draft of air that carried his scent to her. Once he was above her, then he might get a shot.

Stealthily, he made his way to the crest of the bluff, crouching behind a tangle of dead berry vines. He studied the slope below.

Without warning, a twig snapped far to the left of the deer. Matt peered into the underbrush but spotted no movement. After several long moments, he turned his attention back to the doe that by now had browsed into a clearing.

He folded his leg under him and eased down to sit on his foot. Before he cocked the hammer of the Henry, the doe jerked her head erect and peered down the slope to his left.

Matt pivoted and cocked the hammer, searching

the tangled underbrush for whatever had disturbed the doe. When he glanced back, she was feeding once again. He grinned. Whatever had bothered her was no more.

He lined the sights up on her shoulder, and before he could pull the trigger, his head jerked to the side as if someone had struck him with a singletree. Then he heard the crack of a rifle.

Matt felt himself falling from the rim of the bluff to the creek a hundred feet below. The Henry slipped from his grasp.

Chapter Sixteen

When Charley heard the echo of the gunshot, he guessed Matt had downed a deer. Minutes dragged into an hour, and then a second hour. That's when Charley rushed Mary Elizabeth and the boys inside. "I do not know." He pointed to the Sharps leaning against the wall. "Use that, if you must." And then he vanished into the forest.

The white man had no concept of the Comanche predilection for survival. From the time they are toddlers, every lesson given them is to survive, regardless of means. Even in a state of semiconsciousness, the instinctive desire for survival galvanizes the Comanche into action.

When Matt tumbled over the bluff, his childhood

training forced him to grab for the nearest buffer to stop his fall.

Like the claws of an eagle, his fingers grasped the tangle of vines and broke his fall. For long moments he clung to the vines, then feeling the musty breath of ancient caves on his face he lunged forward, instinctively aware that while the opening would protect him from whatever was above, he had no idea what might be awaiting him within.

Moments later, a Tonkawa warrior squatted and peered over the rim of the bluff at the creek far below, noting the hat floating on the ripples on the dark water.

Rising to his feet, he studied the forest around him. He had returned seeking his brother but found only a white man. He grunted. Perhaps his brother would return but the white man was dead. He would never return.

The sun burned at the snow, melting it quickly.

Charley studied their situation. Instinctively, he felt they needed to move from this camp but he couldn't leave without Matt Fields.

Mary Elizabeth looked up at him, her dark eyes filled with anguish. "You think Matt's all right? It's dark outside. He's been gone all day."

All Charley could do was shrug. "Tomorrow, I find him."

Joe frowned up at him. "What if . . . what if you don't find nothing?"

Charley studied the three. "I do as he. I take you to white eyes."

During the night, a dull throbbing in the back of his skull dragged Matt back into a state of semi-consciousness. He opened his eyes, but he could see nothing. He closed his eyes and drifted back into a deep slumber.

Next morning at the same time Charley moved out in his search for Matt, Carson and his men pulled out of Coy's Landing, the crisp morning air brushing over their brutish faces. They pushed their ponies hard.

For a tracker of Charley's ability, cutting Matt's sign was simple, at least, in the beginning. Then he began losing the sign. A knowing grin played over his thin lips. Matt was covering his trail just in case hostile Indians or white men happened to pass this way.

Mid-afternoon the Caddo returned to the cave with the disappointing news he had not found Matt. He squatted by the fire and sipped cassina tea and chewed on a slab of venison.

"Can't we help look for Matt?" Lester looked up at Charley hopefully.

"No." He shook his head. "You stay. Trouble enough with one lost."

The remainder of the day turned up no sign of Matt other than a faint imprint of a moccasin on the edge of a narrow stream. Taking care to study the forest around him, Charley searched a mile upstream. Half a mile downstream, he found Matt's hat, a gray Stetson. A grim frown twisted his swarthy face.

The mood around the fire that night was subdued. Mary Elizabeth wiped at her red-rimmed eyes. "He'll be back. I know he will."

"Yeah," Joe muttered. "He probably just lost the hat. That's all."

"That's it," Lester said. "That's what happened. He just lost it."

Charley studied the three, his usually stoic face soft with tolerance. Lester glanced at Joe, then cut his eyes back to the fire. He had plans of his own.

Carson reined up well before sundown, explaining that he planned to rise early next morning and ease into the area around the massacre.

"Why don't we just go on in and camp there?" Higgins asked.

Carson glowered at him. "Because I don't want them to smell woodsmoke, stupid. That's why!"

Higgins bit his tongue. He knew better than to argue with Carson. But, he told himself, if he ever had the chance to put a slug in the big man, he would.

Next morning, Carson yanked the three from their

bedrolls early and rode out. "I want to be there by sunup."

Ten minutes after the gray of false dawn insinuated itself throughout the forest, they reined up at the site of the massacre.

Higgins pulled out a twist of tobacco and bit off a chunk. "Now what?"

The big man remained motionless, his jaw tilted. He sniffed at the air, but smelled nothing other than the sharp tendrils of cold air. "It was just down the trace that Blacky spotted the kid. I figure they're around here somewhere."

"Maybe they done rode out," Horrells muttered, searching the forest around him.

"Weather's been too bad up until the last couple of days. If they moved out then, we'll find tracks. There ain't been no snow to cover them. We'll spread out and ride in the same direction. Just keep the one on either side in sight. After a couple of miles if we don't cut no sign, we'll move over and come back."

Fifteen minutes after Charley set out on his search for Matt, Lester slipped into his coat and tugged on his hat.

"Where do you think you're going?" Mary Elizabeth demanded, her fists jammed into her hips.

The young boy glared at his sister defiantly. "I'm going to help find Matt, that's where, and don't think you're going to stop me."

Joe climbed to his feet, his freckled face red with anger. "She might not but I sure will. You stay here like Charley said."

Lester narrowed his eyes. "You can't make me."

"We'll just see about that," Joe said, taking a step forward.

Lester kicked the older boy in the shin. When Joe screamed in pain and bent over to grab his shin, Lester shoved him backward, sending the slender youth tumbling into the fire.

In the next instant, the towheaded boy grabbed his spear thrower and burst through the bearskin door. He scrambled up the side of the gully and disappeared into the forest, a wide grin on his face. As soon as he was a short distance from the ancient cave, he darted behind a tree and peered over his back trail.

He saw Joe limp out of the gully followed by Mary Elizabeth. For a moment, he thought they might follow, but then he breathed a sigh of relief when they turned back inside.

Taking a deep breath, Lester looked around, suddenly puzzled as to his next move. He had no idea where to search for Matt. He could be anywhere. Back to the south was the trace. "That's where I'll look first," he muttered, setting off through the forest.

By now, much of the snow had melted, leaving behind cloying mudholes that sucked at his feet. Travel was arduous, and within minutes his breath was growing short and perspiration rolled down his face.

He clenched his teeth and continued plodding toward the winding road.

Far to the east in one of the caves in the face of the bluff, Matt's shivering muscles and chattering teeth cut into his numbed sleep. As he struggled back into the first vestiges of consciousness, he felt the throbbing in the back of his head. Gingerly, he touched his fingers to the knot, feeling the dried blood.

The effort, though slight, exhausted him, and he sagged back onto the dirt and drifted back into semiconsciousness.

Charley widened his search area. Less than fifteen minutes out, he spotted a glimmer beneath the surface of a pond. It was the Yellowboy Henry. He fished it out and studied it. His keen eyes swept upstream, peering into the tangles and shadows.

In the distance, he saw movement. Instantly, he dropped to his knees behind an ancient loblolly pine.

Lester was hiding behind a pine when a snorting horse startled him. The young boy looked around and less than thirty feet distant, a bearded jasper sat on the horse staring at him, his eyes filled with as much surprise as the boy's.

"Boy! You—"

He had no chance to say another word for in one smooth move, Lester lifted the spear thrower and hurled the spear at the rider.

The spear slammed into the rump of the horse, causing the animal to explode into a bucking frenzy. The man cursed at the top of his lungs and jerked on the reins mercilessly.

Lester turned and ran.

Behind him, a voice called out, "Blacky. Look out. A kid's coming at you."

"*Oui!* I catch that one."

Ahead, Lester spotted a downed pine across the narrow creek. He leaped on the pine and raced across the narrow stream, leaping to the ground and pressing up against the thick trunk.

The first voice demanded. "Where'd the brat go?"

"He be around here somewhere. Across the creek."

The young boy's heart thudded against his small chest like a blacksmith's hammer. He swallowed hard and hunkered down as low as he could.

The voices seemed to be fading into the distance. Slowly, he raised his head and peeked over the scaly bark of the pine straight into the black eyes of a sneering cowboy.

"Been waiting for you, boy."

Lester leaped to his feet and made a mad dash into the forest but four horsemen quickly surrounded him. His eyes filled with tears of frustration and anger, he dodged and darted, but each time he turned, another cowpony was in front of him.

Finally, he stopped, his arms hanging limply at his side, his shoulders slumped, and his chin on his chest.

Chapter Seventeen

From deep in the shadows of the ancient forest, Charley One-Horse watched in frustration as one of the riders yanked Lester up behind him and headed south. The Caddo warrior glanced over his shoulder in the direction he had planned to search for Matt. That had to wait. The boy came first.

The owlhoots stayed on the trace, riding easily, slowly, knowing they had an ace in the hole.

Like a wraith, Charley followed. A few miles farther, Carson made camp in a tangle of wild berry vines.

Waiting until they had set up their camp before creeping closer, Charley deliberated several plans to free the boy, but none of them were without danger to the youth. Finally, he contented himself by slipping within earshot to learn of the owlhoots' intentions as they sat around a blazing fire chewing on jerky and drinking rotgut whiskey.

The big man was the one Matt called Carson. He shoved Lester to the ground against a tree and growled. "Try to run, and we'll tie you up tighter than a fritter. You hear me, boy?"

Lester nodded, his lips curled in a surly sneer.

Blacky Dow growled, "So what do we do now, Ed? About the boy, I mean? He ain't going to tell us nothing."

Carson glanced at Dow, then turned his eyes to the forest. He rubbed absently at the arrowhead-shaped scar above his right eye. "Whoever they are out there, they know we got the kid. We could shoot him now, and that would be one out of our hair but that wouldn't solve our problem. There might only be one more out there, or there might be a dozen. We got no way of knowing." He glared at Lester. "And you ain't going to tell us how many, are you, boy?"

Setting his jaw, the youngster shook his head emphatically.

Glaring down at the boy, Carson lifted an eyebrow. "We could beat it out of you."

Lester swallowed hard but remained silent.

With a chuckle, Carson plopped down on his soogan and leaned back against the trunk of an ancient oak. "I don't cotton to whipping up on younkers though my pa never figured that way." He fixed his eyes on Lester. "If I got to shoot you, boy, I will, but I ain't going to whop you none." He turned back to his men. "Stop and figure. We kill them all, we still ain't got the money. What I figure is that we got a choice to make."

"What choice is that?" Higgins leaned forward.

"Money or freedom."

"What do you mean by that, Ed?"

"We kill them all, there ain't no one to say what happened at the wagon train. But, if we do, we ain't got the eight thousand. I say, take the money and get out of here. With my share of the loot, I can disappear forever. I'll take my chances." He paused and surveyed the three gunnies as they pondered his suggestion. "That way I got the best of it all, the money and the freedom—as long as I stay one step ahead of the law."

Dow and Higgins grinned at each other. They nodded agreement as Wes Horrells spoke up. "I'm with you, Ed, but how do we get the money if we can't find them and can't make this one talk?"

Carson's black eyes searched the dark forest. "We'll give them a message."

Higgins frowned. "A message? How do you reckon on doing that?"

Without replying, Carson tore the top from a box of .44 cartridges and laboriously printed: *Eight thousand or the boy dies.*

"There," he muttered when he finished.

Dow arched an eyebrow. It was one thing to write out a message, but an entirely different one in getting it to those with the money. With a faint sneer in his tone, he asked, "How do you reckon getting it to them when we don't know where they is?"

With an amused gleam in his eyes, Carson gestured to the forest. "You think they ain't out there right now, watching us?"

Dow jerked around, his swarthy face wreathed in disbelief. "Out there? Right now? *Mon ami!* How you know?"

Carson chuckled. "Don't believe me? Just walk out there in the shadows and see what happens."

Horrells and Higgins looked at Dow expectantly.

Dow shook his head. "Not me."

"I didn't think so," Carson replied, pushing to his feet and shucking his six-gun.

Fifty feet out from the camp, he wedged the piece of cardboard into the scaly bark of a pine and returned to camp. By the time he squatted in front of the fire and poured another drink, the note had vanished.

Back at the cave, Mary Elizabeth read the note in stunned disbelief. She looked up at Charley. "What eight thousand dollars?"

Charley shrugged. "All I know, I hide gold in tree like Matt says."

Brushing her black hair back from her face, the young woman grimaced. "What are we going to do?"

Rising soundlessly, the Caddo nodded to the door. "I find Matt. Then we know."

Joe cleared his throat. "But, but what if . . ."

"If he dead, then you decide."

The young woman's face grew taut with anguish. "I just want my little brother back."

The forest floor was soggy from the melting snow. Moving slowly, Charley tried to find firm footing so as not to leave any more sign than possible. The first two bands of Tonkawas had ridden out, but that did not mean others were not passing through, bound for the Wichita villages.

Ahead, he spotted the vine-choked face of the sheer bluff, noting the dark openings behind the dead vines. Gingerly, he made his way along the sandy bank. On the far shore, drifts of snow remained, sheltered from the sun by the bluff above.

Suddenly, Charley froze, staring at a dark object protruding an inch or so from the snow. Instantly, he recognized it as the butt of a handgun. He splashed across the creek and pulled the six-shooter from the snow bank. A Colt. One like Matt's.

His blood ran cold. He cleared the snow at the base of the bluff, but found no body. A few feet downstream was the small pond where he had found the Yellowboy.

Without hesitation, Charley waded in up to his waist in the freezing water, but did not find a submerged body. He followed the creek to where it made a bend at the end of the bluff. The creek grew shallow, rippling over rocks, deep enough for a Stetson to float past but not a body. If Matt's body had floated down, the Caddo told himself, it would have caught here.

He looked back at the bluff, his sharp eyes noting the numerous openings behind the spider web of vines. He nodded, a sly smile playing over his thin lips.

Returning to where he found the Colt, he climbed the vines.

The rattling of vines alerted Matt's instinct for survival, pulling him from his semiconscious state. He reached for his revolver but the holster was empty. He shucked his knife and struggled to sit up, facing the opening.

Without warning, a whispered voice muttered, "Do not shoot. I be Charley One-Horse."

For a moment, Matt thought he was hearing things. "What? Who?"

"Charley. Of the Hasinais Caddo."

Thirty minutes later, Matt was squatting in front of the small fire warming himself while Mary Elizabeth gently tended the wound on the back of his head. Next to him lay his gray Stetson. He shivered as his cold body savored the warmth of the fire.

He had read Carson's message and was trying to sort the jumbled thoughts in his head. The one certainty in his mind was they wanted Lester back, and if that meant turning over the gold, it was a small price.

But, he also took into account Carson's cunning. What assurance was there that Carson would not shoot him in the back after getting the eight thousand? The only answer that made sense was to put the leader of the scavengers out in the open where he couldn't afford to try any tricks.

He laid out his plan to the others after explaining that two thousand of the gold was his and Cotton's. The remaining six thousand belonged to those on the wagon train. He paused and nodded to Mary Elizabeth and Joe. "That's you now—and Lester."

Matt continued, "We'll pick the spot for the trade. Charley, you and Joe take the rifles. We'll find you a spot with a clear shot at Carson if he tries to double-cross us."

Mary Elizabeth smiled gratefully at Matt. "Eight thousand dollars is a lot of money. I think it's wonderful of you to give it to Carson for Lester. I'll always be grateful."

Matt scratched at his grizzled beard. "Like I said, only two thousand is mine—well, was mine and Cotton's. The other is from the wagon train."

Tears rimmed her eyes. "Still, I'm grateful."

Joe cleared his throat. "Do—do you really think we'll get out of all of this, Matt?"

Matt laid his hand on the knot on the back of his head. "I'm sure of it, son. We'll get out of this and find a place to start all over. Why, you'll be able to go to school and—"

"Ugh, I can do without school."

Looking up at Mary Elizabeth, Matt winked. "Maybe you once could, but today, a man needs to know his figures to make sure those you deal with won't cheat you. It's a terrible thing to say about people, but seems like more and more sneaky jaspers today are trying to figure out ways to cheat an honest man out of his money. It's in your best interest to be able to figure just a tad better than them."

Joe considered Matt's advice. "Maybe you're right. I got to think on it."

Matt leaned forward. "Good. Now. Here's what we're going to do with Carson."

Chapter Eighteen

Next morning before sunup, Matt, Joe, and Charley were situated some hundred yards from Carson's camp. "Remember," Matt told the Caddo, "as soon as they start moving about, shoot the arrow with the message into that big pine in the middle of the camp. That way they know we're here but they got no idea where."

Blacky Dow rolled out of his soogan and kicked the banked fire to life. As the first flames leaped up into the frigid air, he added several smaller branches. He touched his fingers gingerly to his healing scalp.

Suddenly, there was a whoosh and a thud. He looked around to see a three-foot arrow vibrating in the pine. "Injuns!" He grabbed his six-gun and dropped to his knees.

Blinking the sleep from his eyes, Carson rolled from his blankets and grabbed his Winchester. He glanced at the arrow and spotted the message tied to the shaft. He growled. "Hold it. It ain't Injuns. It's from our friends in the woods."

He scanned the printed words, then looked up. As the message indicated, a lone individual dressed in buckskins stood beside a pine some hundred yards distant. He held a pair of saddlebags in his left hand.

For several moments, the grizzled outlaw studied the slender figure by the pine. "Holster your hoglegs, boys. They got the money, and they want the boy."

Laying his hand on the butt of his six-gun, Horrells muttered, "Tell 'em to bring it on in."

"He wants me and the boy to come out by ourselves. Blacky, you stay close to that Winchester." Carson glared at Lester. "If he tries anything stupid, nail the boy."

Pink Higgins swallowed nervously. "You think he will?"

Carson pursed his thick lips. "No. Jaspers like that one don't give a rip about money when it comes to kids." He chuckled. "Stupid of him, huh?"

Dow spoke up. "Maybe it's just the two of them, Ed. We could kill them both and take the money. Then we'd never have to worry about nothing."

Carson gave a sarcastic snort. "There's more than two. Are you blind? They got an Injun with them for sure. No, we'll play it his way." He gestured to Lester.

"Come here, boy. And you other rogues stand up and keep your six-guns holstered."

Carson held Lester's arm in a death grip as they left the camp.

Matt watched warily, his gray eyes searching for the slightest hint of treachery from any of the other three hombres in camp. They remained motionless.

As Carson drew nearer, he finally recognized Matt. "So, it's you, Fields. I was wondering who was out here."

With a crooked grin, Matt said, "Not just me, Carson. You can't see them but two rifles are trained on you." The big man stiffened but Matt growled, his words hard and cold. "Don't worry. Even with a skunk like you, I'll play the cards straight, but if I ever again find you, you're going to be looking up at daisies."

Carson forced a laugh but the threat in Matt's voice was chilling. He nodded to the saddlebags. "That the gold?"

Matt laid the saddlebags on the soggy leaves on the forest floor, then took a backward step. "Send the boy. When he gets to me, I'll back away."

Carson narrowed his eyes. "How do I know it's the gold? It could be nothing but creek rocks."

With a chuckle, Matt opened one side of the bags and dribbled a few coins on the ground. "My folks never brought me up to lie like yours did you, Carson. Now what are you going to do?"

His black eyes studied Matt. "How do I know you won't back out of the deal?"

"Because I'm not a lying piece of scum like you. Now, you do what I say, or make your play. And I can punch both your eyes out before you clear leather. You don't believe me then get on with it. I'm tired of fooling with you."

A chill like death ran up Carson's spine. He forced an unfelt sneer to his face. He nudged Lester forward. "All right, boy. Get."

With a muffled shout of glee, Lester raced to Matt, who sharply gestured the boy to his left side, keeping his hand poised above the butt of his Colt. "All right, Carson. We're backing away. You get your thirty pieces of silver and hightail it. Come after us and you'll get cut down like the dogs you are."

Carson suppressed the anger flushing through his veins, burning his cheeks. He reminded himself that there was eight thousand dollars waiting for him, and if he played his cards right, for him alone.

He trudged through the snow and mud and retrieved the saddlebags.

Deep within the dark forest, Matt looked on as Carson and his three gunnies broke camp. He watched Carson climb into the saddle on a chestnut with a bald face and ride out.

Moments later, Joe and Charley joined Matt and Lester. Excitement crossed the boys' faces but Charley stared at Matt impassively. He held out the Yellowboy Henry. He knew what the white man had to do.

Matt nodded to Charley. "Take the boys and find another camp. There are one or two caves in the bluff large enough. I'll join you—" Matt froze. Hastily, he motioned for the others to drop to the ground.

To the west, a mere shadow among the giant oak and pine, an Indian brave glided silently.

The four watched breathlessly as the single warrior floated through the forest in the direction of the cave. Charley glanced sharply at Matt, who signaled Charley to remain behind with the boys.

Then, like a phantom, Matt vanished into the forest on the trail of the Indian, cursing his luck. Now, Carson would have to wait, at least until the intent of the lone Indian became evident.

The direction of the warrior told Matt that the brave had an idea of where he was heading. Even if he didn't, if he kept traveling as he was, he'd run across the gully and the cave, and Mary Elizabeth.

From time to time, Matt glanced over his shoulder, expecting to see more warriors on the trail. Each time, he breathed a sigh of relief.

A half-mile from the cave, the warrior—a Tonkawa Matt discerned from the warrior's paint—cut back to the southeast. A slight grin curled Matt's lips when he realized the Tonk would bypass the cave.

Fifteen minutes later, Matt froze as the rich and pungent odor of woodsmoke teased his nostrils.

Ahead, the Tonk had jerked to a halt, sniffing the air.

Matt muttered a soft curse when the warrior headed directly for the cave. Reluctantly, he drew the Henry to his shoulder and sighted along the octagon barrel. He touched the tip of his finger to the trigger.

Just as he started to squeeze, he caught movement out of the corner of his eye. Ahead, the Tonk froze, then dropped into a crouch on the edge of a clearing.

On the opposite side of the clearing crouched a cougar, its teeth bared, its yellow eyes focused on the Tonkawa. His long tail swept back and forth as the beast readied itself for a charge.

The Tonkawa warrior raised a battered muzzleloader to his shoulder and waited.

The cougar crept forward on the spongy forest floor, intent on his prey before him. The big cat's muscles rippled under his tawny skin, signaling an imminent charge.

Matt looked on, his feelings mixed. If the Tonk's shot did not hit its mark, the beast would be on him in an instant, and given the size of the cougar, the warrior, no matter how gallant, was no match for the savage claws and tearing teeth.

Glancing about him, Matt spotted a water-soaked branch about a foot long at his feet. Without hesitation, he grabbed it and hurled it through the air at the cougar. The fragment of branch hit a few feet from the crouching cougar and bounced into the beast's side, startling him and causing him to flee.

The Tonkawa swept the muzzle of his roundballer around at Matt, who had dropped into a crouch behind an ancient pine and lined up the Yellowboy's sights on the warrior. For several strained seconds the two stared at each other, each waiting for the other to make a move.

After several seconds, Matt raised his left hand in a sign of peace.

Slowly, the Tonk lowered his rifle. Matt did the same.

Neither moved. Matt patted his belly and gestured to the west, well away from the butternut tree, then pointed to the warrior.

The warrior shook his head and gestured in the opposite direction toward the river. Matt nodded, and held up his hand once again in a sign of peace, noting that while the Tonk nodded, he did not return the peace sign.

Slowly, the cowpoke took a backward step, a signal that he was continuing on his own journey. A faint smile played over the Tonkawa's lips as he turned and disappeared into the forest in the direction of the river.

Matt looked after him for several moments, then turned and headed in the direction of the false camp he had indicated to the warrior. If he weren't mistaken, the Tonk would swing around and try to slip up on him.

The trick now was to figure out when and where.

Chapter Nineteen

Matt wouldn't have even had time to smoke a Bull Durham before he heard commotion in the forest behind him. Quickly ducking behind a deadfall, Matt studied the silent woods surrounding him, wondering how far Carson had ridden in the last hour. With the snow melted, he would make good time.

Movement to his left caught his attention. Then Charley One-Horse stepped from behind the bole of an ancient live oak. He held the Tonk's muzzleloader over his head.

Matt grimaced, wondering just how long the killing would go on in this part of the country.

Before Matt set out after the four owlhoots, he studied their sign around the camp, noting the bald-faced chestnut Carson rode was missing two nails on the front left shoe.

Later, Carson felt his chestnut begin favoring his left front. He muttered a silent curse. Moments later, he and his three gunnies reined up on the shore of the muddy Sabine River.

Pink Higgins looked over his shoulder down the dark road from which they had emerged. "You know that jasper is coming after the gold, don't you, Ed?"

Wes Horrells and Blacky Dow looked up at Carson narrowly, awaiting his response. Loosing an arc of tobacco onto the red mud at the horses' feet, Carson grunted, "Yep."

"Maybe we shoulda tried to bushwhack him back there," Horrells muttered.

Carson shook his head at the small man's lack of good sense. "And have half a dozen Winchesters cut us down?"

Dow lifted a suspicious eyebrow. "But you said he claimed he only had a couple of hideouts watching us."

"That's what he said, but that hombre was too sure of hisself." He shook his head. "No, he had more." He glanced down to see his pony holding his weight on his right front. He cursed to himself, hoping the broomtail could get him on back to Coy's Landing before going lame.

Higgins cleared his throat. He looked nervously at his boss. "Then, maybe we best split up the take now. If we get scattered, at least we'll have our share." He laid his hand on the butt of his six-gun and glanced at Horrells and Dow, both of whom nodded in agreement and laid their hands on their revolvers.

Carson restrained the rush of anger burning his grizzled cheeks. He eyed Higgins narrowly, noticing each of his compadres was ready to open the show. "I'd reckoned putting it in the safe of one of those schooners at Coy's Landing. We can take the boat all the way down to Galveston and split up the take there. Then we can go our own way, to any port in the world."

Horrells grinned sheepishly. "Not me. I get sick on them boats." Keeping his right hand on the butt of his six-gun, he gestured across the river with his left hand. "I figure on taking my share and heading to Moss Hill over across the river in Louisiana. I got kin there."

Carson held his temper. Then his eyes settled on the long coupled roan Horrells was forking. The horse feared water. He laughed. "You think you're going to swim the river on that knothead? You know yourself, when it comes to water, she's spookier than a grasshopper in a chicken coop."

The smaller man glanced at Dow and Higgins. He stiffened his jaw. "She can make it, don't worry. How about it, Ed? I got two thousand coming."

"Yeah," Higgins said.

For a moment, Carson considered drawing down on them, but he knew he couldn't put lead plums in all three without taking some lead himself. Still, even with Horrells taking his share, that left six thousand on this side of the river. Six might not be as good as eight, but it was better than just a single share. Besides, he told himself. If Fields is following, then breaking up might be the best thing for all of them.

"If that's what you boys want, then that's fine with me."

Horrells grinned. "I'll make a deal with you, Ed. That chestnut of yours is a good swimmer. I'll swap you my roan and a hundred bucks out of the cut I got coming."

For a moment, Carson hesitated. He had not planned on riding the chestnut any farther than Coy's Landing. There he was taking the schooner to Galveston. The animal was going lame. Let Horrells handle the problem. The big man shrugged. "Sure. Why not?"

The two men swapped ponies. Horrells slid his share of the loot into his fringed saddlebags.

Fifteen minutes later, the three watched as Horrells climbed the far bank on the back of the chestnut. He turned and waved, then disappeared into the forest.

Later, Matt studied the tracks on the muddy bank. He spotted the shoe with the two missing nails and followed it until it entered the river. "Carson," he muttered, lifting his gaze to the far bank.

Hurrying back downriver, he studied the remaining sets of tracks along the shoreline. He nodded, convinced Carson had crossed the river.

Upriver around a bend, Matt lashed a few small logs together and pushed into the current, using his legs to propel the small raft through the frigid water to the far shore.

Upon reaching the Louisiana bank, he stomped his feet and rubbed his arms to restore circulation as he studied the tracks emerging from the river. He grinned in satisfaction when he spotted the tracks with the missing nails in the front left shoe.

For the first several miles, the bald-faced chestnut gave Horrells no indication of going lame. His new rider weighed less than half of the former, so the pony carried its burden easily until a few miles outside of Moss Hill before she started limping.

Horrells dismounted and lifted the animal's hoof. He grimaced and cursed Carson. "You lying, sneaky—" He dropped the hoof and looked up into the chestnut's brown eyes.

Horrells was as much a liar and sneak as Carson but he had a soft spot in his black heart for animals. He looked up the trace, recognizing he was only a few miles from his kin's home place. Instead of swinging into the saddle and forcing the already injured animal to carry him, he took the reins over his shoulder and set out up the road, whistling an off-key rendition of "Blue Tail Fly."

Matt squatted in the red soil and studied the sign, puzzled by the fact Carson was now walking instead of riding. The wiry cowpoke frowned. Someone other than Carson was forking the chestnut or else he'd misjudged the man, and from experience, he knew making the wrong judgment about a jasper could plant an hombre six feet under faster than a cat with his tail afire.

Just before dark, Matt spotted a column of smoke drifting into a sky that was quickly becoming overcast. Under the cover of growing darkness, he eased closer to a ramshackle cabin of rawhide and logs. Three or four bone-thin hounds lay on the tumbledown porch beneath a roof threatening to cave in.

Pausing far enough back in the forest so as not to alarm the hounds, Matt studied the cabin. To the side was a barn and corral. Several ponies milled about, but in the darkness Matt couldn't pick out the chestnut.

Backing away, he circled the cabin and slipped into the barn and burrowed in the hay for the night.

An hour after the sun set behind the pine and oak forest, Carson and his remaining two gunnies rode into Coy's Landing. Throughout the day, the grizzled owlhoot had searched for the opportunity to gun both of them down, but the two remained wary, their eyes never leaving their boss.

Finally, Carson shrugged and gave up. If the schooner was still docked, he'd take passage and head down to Galveston. Once in the port city, he'd have time to decide his next destination. After all, two thousand dollars could take him a long way.

After unsaddling their ponies in the corral and driving them into the barn, the three gunnies stomped inside the inn and plopped down in front of the fire with a bottle of whiskey.

While Higgins and Dow were getting themselves drunk, Carson contacted the captain of the schooner *Nell* and booked passage under the name Frank Adams.

Captain Bellows, a slight man with cool-blue eyes that read Carson like a book, announced, "We pull out first thing in the morning, Mr. Adams. Weather's coming. River's high so we should make good time. Galveston in four days, three if we're lucky."

Back in the saloon, Carson sold his pony and gear to the owner of the inn, then ambled over to Dow and Higgins. He poured a drink and held up his glass. "Well, boys, this is our last night. I booked passage on the *Nell*. We're pulling out at first light."

Higgins and Dow looked at each other in surprise. They had decided a few days earlier between themselves that Carson would not hesitate to gun them down for the gold. They had to protect each other, and it had worked.

The two owlhoots relaxed. Dow grinned. "You take care, Ed. You hear?"

"Don't worry about me. Where you old boys heading?"

Dow nodded across the river. "The old folks live over near Evangeline. Me, I go on to New Orleans from there."

"Not me," said Higgins. "I hear over to the west there's a jungle of forest the locals call The Big Thicket. Word is that no lawman dares go in there. Them what do don't never come out."

Carson lifted an eyebrow. "Sounds right exclusive."

Higgins pursed his lips. "One of my uncles told me about it. He come through a few years back a hop and skip ahead of the law. Said that's where he was heading. I figure on going over there and see if I can find that old boy."

"Well, I wish you luck," Carson replied, waving the old Mexican waitress over. "Now, I could use a steak with my whiskey. How about you boys?"

Higgins and Dow grinned at each other. "Sounds good to me."

After their meal and a few more rounds of drinks, Dow passed out. Carson and Higgins helped him to the room he shared with Higgins, then returned to the fireplace.

Carson eyed his drunken partner. Maybe it still wasn't too late to pick up some extra gold.

Chapter Twenty

In a jovial mood, Carson held up a glass of whiskey. "Well, one more drink for me, and I'm hitting the sack out at the schooner. Here's to you, Pink."

The whiskey had turned Higgins' normally flushed face bright red. "Here's to you, Ed. Hope you don't get seasick on that boat."

Carson seized the moment. "Not me. I got a large cabin with a bed, not one of them small bunks like on most boats. You oughta see it."

Higgins staggered to his feet. "I wouldn't mind seeing it at all. Hey, I might even go with you," he slurred.

Downing his drink, Carson rose to his feet. "Come on. I'll show you."

All Carson showed Higgins was a knife in the back. After relieving the older man of his gold, he rolled him into the river. As the current caught the bobbing body, Carson slipped into the corral, saddled Higgins' bay and turned it loose. Back inside the inn, he jotted a note on a slip of brown paper and slipped into Dow's room. The man hadn't moved, which saved his life.

The drunken owlhoot was dead to the world, not even resisting when Carson felt under the mattress for Dow's share of the gold. Within a minute, Carson pocketed the gold, left the note on the floor, and hurried to the schooner.

Next morning, a banging on Carson's cabin door jerked him from a sound sleep. He opened the door to find an incensed Dow glaring up at him. "You seen Pink?"

Carson rubbed his eyes. "How could I? You woke me up. What's wrong?"

The infuriated outlaw launched into a profane harangue of how his onetime partner had stolen his gold, had the nerve to leave a note mocking him, and ridden out during the night.

Carson shook his head in commiseration. "I never would have figured him for that, Blacky. I'd be plumb tickled to help you chase after him but the ship is pulling out at any time."

The curly haired man looked up at Carson in frustration. "That no-account took every last cent I had. Me, when I catch him, I'll skin him alive."

Carson clicked his tongue. "I don't blame you one

bit. It's a shame a jasper don't know who to trust no more. Hold on." He turned back into his cabin, fished in the pockets of his jeans and pulled out five double eagles. "Here you are, Blacky. A hundred bucks. For old time's sake."

Dow gulped. "I—I never expected that, Ed, but thanks. I can use it." His eyes welled with tears. "I'm ashamed to admit it but all the time I thought you was the one after the gold. I never figured it was Pink."

Carson smiled sadly, doing his best to suppress the laughter in his throat. "It's a shame you can't trust folks nowadays, ain't it."

Back north in Louisiana before sunrise, Matt had set half a dozen snares. By mid-morning, he had three live rabbits that he placed in one of the empty feed sacks he had found in the barn.

Overhead, thick gray clouds pushed in from the north, a portent of a coming storm.

Back at the cabin, smoke still poured from the mud and stick chimney, the hounds still lay sprawled on the porch, and none of the horses were missing.

Approaching the cabin from the chimney side, Matt eased to the corner and tossed the open bag containing the rabbits in the middle of the hardpan in front of the porch.

Even before the commotion erupted, he darted back

into the forest so he could get a good look at whoever emerged from the cabin.

When the bag hit the ground, the rabbits exploded from it. The hounds erupted like they'd been hit with a bolt of lightning, bellowing and howling with that long drawn out keening bawl that echoed through the forest as they pursued the dodging and darting rabbits.

Moments later, the cabin emptied. Half a dozen jaspers, so drunk that given three tries none of them could hit the ground with his hat, staggered out. Five wore overalls and ragged woolens. They grabbed onto the posts supporting the porch to keep from falling and tried to focus on the confusion in the yard.

To Matt's chagrin, he failed to spot Carson, instead recognizing the sixth one as Wes Horrells, the runt of the gang. He muttered a curse, realizing instantly that Carson had somehow swapped ponies and was now in all probability chugging down rotgut whiskey all snug and comfortable in front of a blazing fireplace down in Coy's Landing.

He considered the situation. If this one had split from Carson, then obviously the gold had been divided. He cut his eyes to the west in the direction of the Sabine River.

When one of the jaspers suddenly collapsed to the porch, Matt made up his mind. Shucking his Colt, he planted a slug in the hand-hewn log porch, ripping up a chunk of pine and getting everyone's undivided attention.

"Take it easy, boys. I don't aim to hurt no one, but on the other hand it wouldn't hurt my sleep none if I put a couple of windows through any of you to let the sunlight in."

As one, they leaned forward, swaying on their feet in an effort to focus on him. The older one, his thick beard covering his angular face, slurred, "Who in the Sam Hill are you?"

"Ask that one there." He gestured to Horrells.

The others jerked their heads around. The older one mumbled, "All right, Wes. Who is this hombre?"

Sobering quickly, Horrells shook his head. "I ain't never seen him. I got no idea."

Matt cocked the hammer on his Colt and took a step forward. "You're a liar, Wes. I don't know who these folks are but unless you shuck up your share of the eight thousand, you're a dead man."

One of the drunks shook his head. "Eight thousand? How in the blazes did you ever come into that much money?"

Horrells shook his head emphatically. "It ain't eight thousand. Not even two thousand. I had to pay for a horse—one that went lame on me," he added with a hint of injured pride.

"Two thousand? Is that what you got in them saddlebags in there? Two thousand?" snarled the older jasper. "And you didn't tell us nothing about it? What kind of kin are you not to include your relations in on your good luck?"

"Yeah, Cousin Wes," muttered one of the younger men. "Here we are sharing what little we all got, and you are blasted well holding out on us. Ain't that right, Pa?"

The older man stepped forward. "Your ma, my sainted sister, would roll over in her grave to know just how much of a cheat her son turned out to be." He stepped forward and slapped Horrells across the face.

His face twisted in anger. With a howl of rage, he leaped on the older man, flailing his arms and cursing at the top of his lungs.

For a moment, his cousins looked on, then jumped in to pull Horrells off their pa.

Pulling a knife, Horrells turned on his cousins.

While they were fighting, Matt darted inside the cabin and spotted saddlebags trimmed with leather fringe. He opened one pocket and grinned when he saw the gold coins. As an afterthought, he stuck a slab of bacon in the other pocket.

At the edge of the forest, he paused and looked back in time to see three of the brothers holding Horrells on the ground just as another cousin drove a knife into the struggling man's chest.

Turning on his heel, Matt vanished into the forest. He had considered taking a pony from the corral but decided he could dissolve into the underbrush easier on foot.

Before he had covered fifty yards, Matt heard a howl of anger go up from behind. He grinned to himself. They'd discovered the missing gold.

Shouts carried through the pine and oak forest. From their echoes, Matt guessed Horrells' kin had split up and headed in different directions.

Moving like a wraith, Matt sped toward the river, knowing when they found his sign they would follow. When he reached the muddy river, he headed south along the east shore, searching for a means to dissuade any pursuers.

Half a mile downriver, he found a tangle of wild grapevines.

Guessing Horrells' kin were trackers enough to follow his sign, Matt quickly cut some vines, looped them around a heavy log, then hoisted it over the trail. Deftly, he set a trigger across the path so that when it was sprung, the log would swing down from its lofty height and in addition to cold-cocking whoever was pursuing, would probably take out a half-dozen teeth.

Then Matt cut back to the river.

Thirty minutes later, Finas cackled when he stared at the tracks in the mud. He had already made plans for the gold, and none of them included his pa or his brothers. He flexed his fingers about the butt of his six-gun.

If his moldy brain could have analyzed and synthesized the long-term results of his decision, he probably would have made a different one. But Finas could barely see one day ahead just as he barely saw the log before it hit him.

After crossing the Sabine, Matt studied the two-day-old sign. Overhead, the clouds had thickened and the wind was coming in gusts. He glanced back to the west, wondering about the others. His stomach growled. He couldn't remember the last time he'd eaten.

He shrugged down into his mackinaw. Best move for him was to find a snug place for the night. If his hunch was right, this could be a whopper of a storm.

Drifting into the forest, he spotted a twisting gully with several cutbanks, all too small to offer any protection. Moving rapidly, Matt followed the wash toward its junction with another but smaller river.

He grinned when he spotted a cutbank five feet high where the runoff had carved out a hollow beneath. If the approaching storm were what he thought, snow would fill most of the wash, but his cubbyhole on the north side of the gully would offer more than sufficient protection. Hastily he gathered wood for a fire. With the slab of bacon to fill his belly, he could weather whatever nature threw at him.

Chapter Twenty-one

The storm blew in around midnight. Matt put a couple of more branches on the fire, pulled his coat tighter around him, and lay back under the overhang.

With the wind howling and the snowfall thickening, sleep evaded him.

More than once, he had found himself in life-and-death predicaments, but from the time he was taken by the Apache he always had managed to live through them.

He had no idea how old he was when the Apache murdered his parents and carried him off. He guessed maybe three or four. He did remember the long journey the next spring to a part of the country he later learned was the Texas Panhandle where he was sold to Buffalo Hump, a respected warrior and leader of the Penateka Comanche.

Buffalo Hump's son had been slain, and his grief-stricken wife pleaded for another son.

Matt shook his head slowly as he stared into the mesmerizing flames of the small fire. Comanche life was hard, but he had been treated the same as the other young boys his age.

After a few years when he was old enough, he accompanied war parties as one of a half-dozen young Comanches who served as jinglers—horse wranglers whose only job was to herd the horses at night and trail the extra ponies during the day.

He could still remember the jubilation in the village when they returned from their first raid. And with growing expectations, Matt looked forward to the next.

The success and rewards of the raid filled them with confidence and enthusiasm. Within weeks, the war party moved out again, this time planning to hit settlements along the far western outposts on the Texas frontier all the way to the Gulf of Mexico.

During one battle near Communion Creek, a small band of white men, spurring to the sounds of the fighting in the settlement, came upon the jinglers.

Matt grabbed a club and charged one of them, but the rider rode him down, striking him unconscious and knocking him into a brush-filled arroyo.

A gust of snow swept under the cutbank and into Matt's thoughts. He fed a couple of more branches to the fire and eased farther back into the hollow.

Fumbling inside his coat, he fished out the Bull Durham and built a cigarette. As the wind whipped the smoke away, he stared back into the flames, remembering how he had awakened later that day in the arroyo and started walking. Later, he stumbled onto some trappers and accompanied them back to Camp Perry where he joined a sideshow. Over the next few years, he became expert with both rifle and six-gun.

And then the war came along. Yankees called it the War of the Rebellion; the Southerners, the War of Secession or the War for States' Rights.

By then, Matt had been doing the work of a man for years. When the sideshow folded, Matt joined the Texas Cavalry, where he met Cotton Wills. The two, neither having family, became instant compadres, serving together throughout the war.

Matt's eyes grew cold and his jaw hard when he remembered how Cotton had survived two thousand miles of mud and rain and a dozen bloody battles in four years only to be gunned down by a backshooter like Ed Carson.

The storm lasted until mid-morning. Before Matt pushed out, he glanced over his shoulder to the northwest, wondering how Charley and the others were doing. They had plenty of grub, and Mary Elizabeth had turned into a fair cook. With the grub and the firepower, and Charley One-Horse's cunning, Matt knew they were well protected. He chuckled, and to his surprise, found himself wishing he was with them.

First things first, he thought, pulling his coat about him and pushing out. He trudged through the snow to within sight of the road before he turned south.

He reached Coy's Landing just after dark.

There, he learned from the proprietor that one of the three had taken the schooner down to Galveston. "What about the other two?"

Pausing in wiping down his bar, the inn owner hitched up his trousers over his expansive belly and sucked on a tooth thoughtfully. "Well, sir, that's mighty interesting. One of them, a short black-haired man that talked like one of them Frenchies from Louisiana claimed one of his friends by the name of Higgins stole a heap of money and rode out during the night." He shrugged. "I can't say for sure if he did or not but that Higgins jasper's horse and saddle was gone, so I reckon the little French hombre was right."

Matt outfitted himself with a horse, saddle, and few supplies with the seventy dollars he had in his moneybelt. He rode out the next morning at false dawn, heading south to Pendleton's Trading Post and then on down to Sabine Town.

Throughout the day, he met a handful of travelers heading for Coy's Landing. Though he inquired if they had encountered a hombre of Blacky Dow's description, he wasn't surprised when they had not. Dow probably reached the downriver port the night before.

By sunset the clouds had blown away, and the western sky boasted a brilliant canvas of scarlets and purples. Matt pulled into a livery at Sabine Town and stabled his pony. When he paid his bill, he told the liveryman he was meeting his cousin. He described Blacky, but the wizened old man just shook his head. "There be three more liveries hereabouts. One of them old boys might have seen the feller."

"Nope. No one like that," said the last of the liverymen.

Matt glanced at the stars filling the clear sky. "Getting late. Reckon I'll find a spot to bunk tonight and start looking in the morning."

The old liveryman cackled. "Best place is the Hog's Head Inn down the street yonder. They change linens at least once a week. Only problem is it's next to the Sabine Saloon, and that place gets mighty loud at times."

With a chuckle, Matt thanked him. "Tired as I am, I could sleep through a flood."

The inn and the saloon shared a common wall with a double-wide doorway between the two establishments. Matt glanced through the door at the crowded saloon as he strode through the lobby to the front desk.

* * *

In the saloon, Blacky Dow froze when he spotted Matt with the fringed saddlebags over one shoulder. Hastily, he ducked his head and peered from beneath the brim of his hat while Matt checked in.

His brain raced. *What is that one doing here?* Then he grunted. *The gold! What else?* His heart pounded in his chest. He drew the back of his hand across his dry lips. *Don't get flustered,* he told himself. *All you got to do is light a shuck out of here.* Suddenly, he froze, remembering the fringed saddlebags over the jasper's shoulder. Horrells' saddlebags.

His eyes narrowed as Matt climbed the stairs to the second floor. If that jasper had Horrells' saddlebags, then he probably had Horrells' share of the gold. A sneer played over his swarthy face. He sipped his whiskey. All he had to do was keep a sharp eye and bide his time.

Ten minutes later, Matt left the inn and headed across the muddy street to the Sabine Café without the saddlebags. As soon as the lanky cowpoke entered the café, Dow glanced at the check-in desk. The clerk was gone. With a leering grin, Dow hurried to the counter and checked the register.

Matt Fields, Room 207.

Across the street, Matt grinned when he saw the diminutive owlhoot start up the stairs. His Comanche-trained eyes had not missed the hardcase in the saloon.

* * *

With a furtive glance over his shoulder, Dow bounded up the stairs. Unknown to him, the desk clerk returned just as Dow topped the stairs. The slender man hurried from the inn in search of the sheriff.

Two oil lamps cast the narrow hall in flickering shadows. As the bushwhacker expected, the door was locked. Using his skinning knife, he quickly jimmied the door and slipped inside.

It was blacker than his own heart, so he struck a lucifer and touched it to the candle on the dresser. As soon as the dim light filled the room Dow spotted the saddlebags, but to his chagrin they were empty.

"Blast," he muttered, glaring in the direction of the café. "That means he's got it on him."

He slung the saddlebags against the wall and yanked the door open. He froze. The next thing he knew, a knotted fist slammed him between the eyes, sending him tumbling to the floor.

When he awakened, Matt was sitting on the edge of the bed, calmly smoking a Bull Durham. Dow groaned and laid his fingers on his nose. He felt stickiness on his chin and throat. He struggled to sit up, at the same time reaching for his handgun. It was missing.

"Forget it. It's on the bed," Matt drawled. "You never learn, do you? Thieves like you always end up dead on the side of the road, in the middle of the woods, or in somebody's hotel room and without a name for your headstone."

Dow's eyes grew wide. "What are you going to do to me?"

Inhaling shallowly, Matt let the smoke drift up past his eyes. "I should kill you. You killed my partner and stole our money, money we'd worked for."

Beads of sweat popped out on the Frenchman's forehead. He dragged his tongue over his lips, wetting them. "Not me. I was there, but it was Ed and Pink that did all the killing. That's the gospel."

Matt grinned. "You wouldn't know gospel if you heard it. Now, where's the others? Tell me, and I might let you live another day."

Dow swallowed hard. "Me, I don't know. Ed—that one—he take a boat to Galveston. I thought Pink stole my money. When me, I wake up, the money was gone and he was gone. His horse was missing but I found the horse, saddle and all, a few miles south. Me, I got no idea where he is."

The first part of his story jibed with that of the proprietor back at Coy's Landing. Matt studied the trembling man coldly. He had killed during the war but that was different, a heap different.

Dow's eyes shifted from Matt's face to the Colt at his side then to his own six-gun in the middle of the bed, measuring his chances.

A sharp knock at the door interrupted them. A voice called out. "This is Sheriff Palmer. Is everything all right in there? I heard there might be a thief ransacking the rooms up here."

With a chuckle, Matt opened the door. “Come in, Sheriff.” He nodded to Dow. “This is your man.”

The sheriff growled, “Get up you.”

Slowly, Dow pushed to his feet, then with a burst of surprising speed leaped between the two men, knocking them both aside.

Matt fell back on the bed. The sheriff bounced off the wall and rushed from the room.

In the next instant, a sharp crack and a terrified scream echoed down the hall. Matt hurried out and halted when he saw the sheriff standing at a shattered railing and staring into the lobby below.

Sheriff Palmer glanced at Matt when the lean cowboy stopped at his side. “Might as well get it this way as by a rope.” He nodded to the unnatural angle of Dow’s head. “A busted neck is a busted neck.”

Matt grunted.

The sheriff drawled. “All right, cowboy. Let’s save us time. Tell me what this is all about.”

Chapter Twenty-two

Next morning before Matt rode out of Sabine Town for Galveston, he was drawn to the river's edge by a gathering of citizens. The sheriff looked up at Matt. "Take a look. My deputy found this one floating down the river. From the story you told me last night, this jasper might be one of them you was looking for?"

The body was so distended and mutilated that identification was next to impossible except for the red hair. "Looks like him. About the right height. And the red hair."

"Well, he ain't got nothing on him with a name. No money. Just another poor jasper who'll ride through the hereafter with no handle."

"They called him Pink Higgins."

"Reckon that's what we'll use then."

Matt studied the body, telling himself that only one of the four responsible for the death of his partner remained. And sooner or later, he'd run down Ed Carson. He fished a half eagle from his pocket. "Here. This'll bury him."

On the north side of Galveston Bay three days later, Matt reined up and peered across the rippling gray waters at the city sprawled on the narrow island. Few souls lived there who were not after an unwary jasper's money.

Pulling off the road, he removed his saddlebags and except for a hundred dollars, cached them and the gold in a hollow tree stump, after which he dragged some dead berry vines around it.

He swung back into the saddle and studied the bay before him. It was a day's ride around the bay to Galveston. "All right, boy. Let's us ride on in."

The next day in the seaport city, Matt sold his horse and gear, not knowing just where his search would take him.

The *Nell* had docked two days earlier, disembarking all of her passengers. Since that time, over a dozen ships had put out, all to distant parts of the globe.

According to Captain Bellows' wife, the captain had gone to the line's main office in Houston. He was due back in on Wednesday.

For the next two days, which were blustery and

cold as if Mother Nature was readying her muscle for another hard blow, Matt went from one maritime line to the next. Carson's name failed to appear on the manifests of any ship that had put out to sea, but as one sympathetic clerk opined at the Far East Traders' Line on the Strand, "Half of our passengers use names other than their own."

Outside, the wind picked up, and a light mist began to fall, an icy drizzle that drove the chill into a body's bones. Matt looked up and down the street filled with men and women of every description, all scurrying to a warm and snug harbor of their own, safe from the coming weather.

He fell in with the crowd, wondering if Captain Bellows had yet returned. He turned down a dark street to a small but neat cottage surrounded by lush trees and thick shrubs.

Bellows invited Matt inside but the buckskinned cowboy declined, glancing at the fine furniture in the neatly kept house. "All I need to know, Captain, is if the gent you took on in Coy's Landing might have mentioned his intentions once he hit Galveston? He goes by the handle of Ed Carson. Tall man, couple inches taller than me and fifty pounds heavier. Has a scar over his right eye."

The captain studied Matt with his clear blue eyes as he had studied Carson a week earlier. "I had no passenger by that name, sir." Before Matt could reply, the sharp-eyed old man continued. "But I did take a gent of that description on at Coy's Landing along with two or three other passengers. Called himself Frank Adams."

Matt's pulse speeded up. "Did he give any idea of his destination?"

Captain Bellows paused, pursing his lips. "That important to you, boy?"

"Mighty important, Captain. Carson backshot my partner when him and his band of scavengers wiped out a wagon train up to the north."

A frown knit the smaller man's forehead. "What about the others with him?"

A wry grin curled one side of Matt's lips. "He's the only one left, Captain."

Bellows' eyes twinkled. "I have no idea if he followed through with it, but he asked directions to the Oriental Clipper Lines. Said he had a hankering to see China."

Matt grimaced and muttered a soft curse.

"Don't go and get yourself all worked up, boy. The *Jade Clipper* goes out once a month. The next one due out is"—he slipped a gold pocket watch from his vest and popped the top—"yep, tomorrow evening on the tide." He glanced up at the sky. "If the weather's not too bad."

The wiry cowpoke couldn't believe his luck. The Oriental Clipper Lines was one of the lines he had visited. He had even spotted the *Jade Clipper* bobbing alongside the dock. "I don't suppose you have any notion of where he's staying?"

The older man shook his head. "Sorry."

Matt extended his hand. "I'm obliged to you, Captain."

"Good luck." He stood at the door until Matt turned the corner at the gate of the picket fence. He closed the door, failing to catch a glimpse of three ghostly figures creeping after Matt.

The wind blew harder, and the mist intensified into a steady cold rain, but Matt's soaring hopes ignored the chill of the growing weather.

Pulling his mackinaw around his neck and tugging his Stetson down over his ears, he ducked his head into the wind and hurried down streets lit dimly by lamp flames dancing wildly in the wind.

After crossing Broadway, he cut toward the docks, planning on checking with the clipper to see if Carson was already on board. If he wasn't, then it would simply be a matter of waiting until the cold-blooded killer showed up to board next morning.

The howling wind and the driving rain blocked all sound but its own.

That's why Matt didn't hear the pounding of feet until they were right on top of him. He felt a heavy blow to his side and another to his back, and then his head exploded.

* * *

Kneeling on the edge of the dark street, the three muggers quickly stripped Matt of his Colt and the gold in his pockets.

One of the thugs looked up at his accomplices, whose faces were hidden beneath the brims of their hats, and whistled. "Look at that gold. Carson didn't say nothing about that."

"Exactly," muttered the second thug. "And he don't need to know nothing about it either. You understand?"

The other two muggers grinned at each other. "Yeah, Whisk. We understand."

Whisk, so named for his deft fingers whisking wallets from unsuspecting marks' pockets, shoved the gold in his pocket. "All right. Now, let's toss this body in the water."

Three hundred miles to the north, Mary Elizabeth jerked awake, her breath coming in short gasps. She stared at the tiny glimmers of light flickering on the roof of the cave.

From beyond the canvas drape separating her pallet from the other, Charley One-Horse whispered, "What is trouble?"

She relaxed, realizing her nightmare of Matt being killed was only a dream. "No, no," she replied softly, "only a bad dream."

Pulling her blanket up around her throat, she whispered a short prayer for Matt, realizing her feelings for him ran deeper than she had thought.

Chapter Twenty-three

The shock of hitting the water jerked Matt from the numbed state in which the attack had left him. He opened his lips to shout for help but water poured down his throat, choking him. He coughed and sputtered, flailing out with his arms.

A sudden excruciating pain in his back and side doubled him into a ball, and he found himself sinking below the icy black water. Somewhere deep in the recesses of his brain, there appeared the image of Mary Elizabeth kneeling by the small fire. Adrenaline coursed through his veins.

Against searing pain that grated against the raw nerves screaming in his body, Matt forced himself back to the surface, using only his right arm. The muscles in his left arm refused to respond to the signals his frantic brain was sending.

Finally, he reached the surface and looked around, but the gusting wind was battering the bay with five-foot waves. The driving rain blinded him.

With no idea of the direction safety lay, he swam, knowing that was his only hope. The keen pain in his back and side slowly brought into focus the jumbled thoughts in his head.

How long he swam, he had no idea. The waves grew smaller, and the wind let some, but the howling and shrieking remained. Suddenly, his fingers touched wood. Like claws, his numbed fingers scrabbled for a hold. He felt a halyard and locked his fingers around it.

An irate voice shouted, "Who's out there? Get off my vessel, or I'll blow your head off."

Moments later, a light appeared above and a wrinkled face, molded craggy and rugged by a lifetime at sea, peered down at him. "Well, I'll be," he muttered. Then over his shoulder, he called out, "Monk. Get your worthless hide out here."

Matt had no idea when the storm blew away. When he awakened two days later, he stared into an overhead of thick beams in a darkened hold. He tried to move but two shards of pain, one on either side of his wiry body, lanced through him.

He arched his back and groaned.

A black man looked around from the small metal stove and peered into Matt's face. "Reckon he's waking up, Mr. Coop."

Cooper Williams peered through the shadows at the stirring man. "Looks thataway, Monk. Why don't you get some rest? You been looking after that lubber for two days now."

Wearing a turtleneck sweater and heavy duck trousers, Monk stretched his massive arms over his head and yawned. His resonant voice carried a teasing edge. "Sure you can handle him, Mr. Coop?"

Coop shot Monk a disgusted look. "I helped you, didn't I? If I can handle a hardhead like you, I can handle someone like him."

Monk chuckled. "Yes, sir. I reckon you can." The large man ducked through the hatchway and disappeared into the bowels of the ship.

Coop shuffled over to Matt and studied the unconscious man's face. Pain had wrenched it gaunt and pale, but there was a hint of determination in the man's jaw that told the old sailor that this was one jasper who wasn't going away without a fight.

He bathed the sweat from Matt's face. Matt's eyes flickered, so Coop spooned up a small bowl of fish broth from a pot on the top of the small metal stove. Patiently over the next few minutes, he managed to worry several spoonfuls of the hot liquid down Matt's throat.

Slowly, the strain that had drawn Matt's features

taut began, like the tide, to ebb, and his face relaxed. Finally, he slipped back into a deep slumber.

While he slept, Coop inspected the bandages on the wounds. No fresh blood, which likely meant the deadly blades had hit nothing major.

The old man leaned back and reached into the overhead. He pulled out a bottle of rum from a shelf and filled a cup. Leaning back, he studied the unconscious man.

"Reckon you got some kind of story to tell, feller. I'm looking forward to hearing about it." He gulped the rum, dragged the back of his hand over his lips, and glancing furtively at the open hatchway in the bulkhead, poured another. He gulped it down quickly. It would never do for Monk to catch him drinking two rums. His old friend would nag at him for the next month.

By now, the warmth of the rum was filling his belly, radiating through his body. He poured a third and leaned back, staring unseeing at Matt and thinking back of the eighty-odd years he had lived on the sea. "Yep, Cooper Williams. You is a mighty lucky old salt to have family like old Monk."

Matt awakened next morning before sunrise. He lay staring into the shadows in the overhead, feeling the gentle rocking of the vessel beneath him.

The small fire in the iron stove filled the small cabin with warmth. Moments later, a lantern appeared in the open hatchway and a wizened man who seemed to roll when he walked, entered.

"Well, now, look who's awake. Monk and me had been wondering if you was planning on hibernating until come spring." He hung the lantern on a hook in an overhead beam and plopped down in a chair beside the bunk. "How you feeling?"

"I'm not sure," Matt muttered, turning his head and wincing at the slight stab of pain at the movement. "Where am I?"

Coop gestured to the cabin. "Aboard the *Tahiti Tradewind,* a Ballyhoo schooner that's been my home for the last sixty years." He patted the edge of the bunk gently. "She's old but she's served me right good. Built out of live oak and hickory wood. Last a lifetime." He cackled. "Got another twenty years to go."

Matt closed his eyes and drew a deep breath. "How long have I been here?" He felt sweat popping out on his face.

"Since the night of the storm. Let's see, that'd be maybe three days ago."

The wiry cowboy's fevered brain struggled to process the information. Three days. That meant Ed Carson had a two-day start on him. He leaned forward, then groaned and sagged back in the bunk.

He awakened later that day, staring up at a solidly built black man staring down at him. From somewhere in the fuzzy recesses of his head, Matt remembered a black man tending him. He dragged the tip of his tongue over his dry lips, wetting them.

"How you be feeling?"

Matt nodded. "Reckon I'm going to live."

Monk chuckled. "Me and Mr. Coop is right glad to hear that." He offered Matt a dipper of water. Matt tried to hold his head up, but the strain revived the sharp pain radiating from his wounds. Gently, Monk held Matt's head while the exhausted man drank greedily.

A few minutes later, Coop entered with a bowl of thick broth with chunks of beef in it. "About time to get something solid down your gullet," he said, nodding to Monk to prop pillows behind Matt so he could sit. "What do they call you?"

Matt tried to chuckle, but the effort caused him to grimace. "My friends call me Matt Fields. My enemies . . . well, I don't reckon you'd care to hear what they call me."

Coop cackled. "I got the same enemies, boy. Now, you think you can feed yourself while I look at your wounds?"

Matt's hand trembled when he reached for the spoon. "I can try."

Monk took the spoon from Matt's shaking fingers. "Here. Let Monk do that for you."

Coop looked up at the big man and nodded. "Monk."

A grin as wide as the Sabine River revealed a set

of glistening white teeth that contrasted sharply with his blue-black skin. "You welcome, Mr. Coop."

The old sailor grunted as he inspected the wounds. "You was lucky you had that mackinaw on. If the knives had gone any deeper you might not be here right now. As it is, they look right healthy to me, at least as healthy as knife wounds can look." He replaced the bandages. "Who did this to you, Matt?"

"I'm not sure, but I been looking for a hombre that goes by the handle Ed Carson or Frank Adams. He's the only one I know has got any reason to see me dead."

"Carson, huh? Don't know the lubber."

"He took passage on the *Jade Clipper* Thursday. Big man. Scar over his right eye."

Coop arched an eyebrow. "If he was on the *Clipper,* then he piled up on Boliver Peninsula back to the north. The storm had passed but the weather was still touchy. The captain sailed. When he hit the cut, he lost his steering and the winds pushed him ashore."

A surge of excitement coursed through Matt's veins. He reached to throw the covers from him, but clenched his teeth and doubled over with an agonizing groan.

"Easy, boy, easy. You got to give them cuts time to heal."

Biting his lip until it bled, he managed to gasp out, "I can't. Carson will disappear. I've got to find him."

Gently, Coop pushed Matt back on his bunk. "Son,

you ain't got the strength to walk out of this here cabin, much less go gallivanting after some jasper what's likely a hundred miles from here by now." He shook his head. "Tell you what. Describe this lubber to us. Monk will see if he can find him for you." He turned to the black man. "That okay with you?"

Monk nodded. "Yessir, Mr. Coop."

Coop turned to Matt. "How about it? All right with you?"

Matt smiled gratefully, closed his eyes, and sagged back in his bunk, asleep before his head touched the pillow.

Chapter Twenty-four

Ed Carson was holding on to the rail of the *Jade Clipper* when she ground ashore on Boliver Peninsula across the bay from Galveston. He studied his situation. The weather was ferocious and cold but he had weathered several hurricanes with winds more than double the fifty-mile-per-hour gusts pounding the ship now.

That the vessel was a total loss was obvious, but she was in no danger of breaking up. He rolled his massive shoulders and studied the frantic passengers scrambling ashore.

The smart move was to wait out the storm on the clipper. After it blew over, he could make his move. He glanced over his shoulder toward Galveston. With Matt Fields taken care of, he had no reason to hurry.

Still, he told himself, there's always a chance the hombre survived. The sleazy pack of muggers he'd hired admitted they had not seen the dead body. "But, he be dead, sure enough," whined one of them. "Me and Squid here put our blades in him up to the handle. He was bleeding like a gutted mackerel when he hit the water. Don't you be worrying, Mr. Carson, sir. That one, he be knocking on Davy Jones' locker."

By noon the next day, the weather had abated somewhat, but the violent waves scouring the beach clean were too large to breach by boat, forcing the passengers to endure the long trek around Galveston Bay to the city.

On the shore beyond the beached ship, several locals, mimicking the practices of the Yankee carpetbaggers, seized the opportunity to shakedown the desperate passengers by offering horses and carriages at three times the going rate.

Packing his warbags, Carson clambered down the ladder and reluctantly paid a hundred and fifty dollars for a spavined sorrel that went lame within thirty minutes.

An hour later, Carson spotted a tendril of smoke drifting into the pale blue sky back to the north, near East Galveston Bay, a finger of water running back to the east twenty-five miles, a bay that had harbored more than its share of pirates and rum smugglers over the decades.

At a melon farm, he swapped off his broken-down sorrel for a roan and gave the farmer a hundred dollars to boot. In addition, he got directions that would take him to Anahuac and then on around Galveston Bay to the Oriental Clipper's branch office in Houston where he could take passage to China once again. Besides, he told himself, the company owed him the fare, and they blasted well would make it right if they knew what was good for them.

As soon as the weather permitted, salvage ships rushed out of Galveston, anxious to retrieve their share of the cargo. By the time Matt regained consciousness, the wreck of the *Jade Clipper* was only a curious incident of the past.

Drifting down on the docks, Monk heard talk of the wreck. Half of the passengers had returned to Galveston to await another passage. Mingling among them, offering to tote their bags, he'd made subtle inquiries of Ed Carson or Frank Adams. No one knew either man.

Each night, Monk returned to the schooner with disappointing news. The fourth night, luck smiled on him at the Jug O' Rum on Sixth Street near the docks. A dimly lit grog shop, it was a hangout for deckhands, roustabouts, and waterdogs from every country in the world.

Pausing with his cup of rum at his lips, a lime juicer peered across the table at Monk. "Never got the bloke's name but he was tall. Kept to hisself on the boat, he did. And he had the evil eye. And a scar over that eye."

Monk listened in rapt attention.

Back in the schooner, Matt felt his pulse race as Monk related the information he had picked up, especially about the scar. He leaned forward. "Where did he say this jasper went?"

Monk pointed to the east. "The limey say the man ride east along the peninsula."

Matt tried to throw his legs over the edge of the bunk, but a stab of pain hit him in the side, doubling him over. Captain Coop laid his hand on the younger man's shoulder and eased him back down on his bunk. "Easy, boy, easy. You're healing, but don't get ahead of yourself. Let me take a look to make sure you didn't tear nothing open."

Cold sweat drenched his pale face. He sagged back on the pillow, exhausted, his hopes of running down Carson beginning to fade.

Moments later, Coop grunted. "You're okay. Just don't move too sudden-like, you hear?"

Matt nodded. "I hear."

That night, Matt dreamed of Mary Elizabeth and the others. The plaintive mourning of the foghorns awakened him during the early morning hours. He lay staring into the darkness.

Gingerly, he eased his legs over the side of the bunk and with the help of the overhead beam, rose to his feet. He stood unsteadily for several moments, before plopping back down on his bunk.

Next morning, Monk was nowhere to be seen. When Matt inquired of Coop, the old captain nodded to Boliver. "He's over there trying to get a heading on that Carson lubber you been chasing."

Matt smiled gratefully over the cup of coffee in his hand. "I'm mighty obliged for all you and Monk done for me, Captain Coop."

Coop brushed it off. "You'd of done the same."

Matt thought of Charley One-Horse, and knew the captain was right.

Day by day as Matt's strength returned, he grew more restless, as did his concern for Mary Elizabeth and the others. He reminded himself of Charley's promise. The Caddo would die before he broke his word. Still, Matt told himself, he'd be mighty glad when this was over and he returned to the cave up north.

On the third day after Monk's departure, a skiff bumped up against the starboard bow and a voice that Matt recognized as Monk's called for a line.

He smiled broadly as he climbed aboard. "Your man is over to Houston, Matt."

Captain Coop ignored the statement. "You all right, Monk? You look a little peaked."

Monk's grin broadened. "No, sir, Mr. Coop. I's fine."

The old man grunted brusquely. "Well, then, don't keep us standing out here in the cold. Come on down to the galley and tell us what you found."

Cupping his steaming coffee with his massive hands, Monk looked at Coop. "You knows that melon farmer, Mr. Picard, where we buys them melons we sell over in Houston?"

Coop nodded. "What about him?"

"He sold a big man a horse. Said he wanted to know how to get to Houston on horseback." Monk sipped the coffee. "I followed him on up to Anahuac where he swap off that nag Picard sold him. He was still heading to Houston."

"How do you know he was the one Matt's after?"

Monk touched a finger to his forehead over his right eye. "The melon farmer said he had a scar right here."

The old captain grinned at Matt. "A few more days and you'll be ready to travel."

Matt agreed, but as quickly as the smile had come to his lips, it faded.

"What's the matter? I thought you'd be right pleased to hear the news."

"I am, I am." Matt knit his brow. "But how am I going to find him in a place like Houston?"

Coop shrugged. "Reckon the same way you found him here in Galveston except you got one advantage now."

"How's that?"

"You know where he wants to go. The Oriental Clipper Lines has a branch in Houston. Were I you, that'd be the first place I'd look. Besides, didn't you say Captain Bellows told you the Clipper Lines only sails for China once a month?"

A broad grin erased the frown on Matt's face. "Yep, he sure did. He most certainly did."

"First thing we got to do," Coop added, eyeing Matt's thin buckskins, "is put you into some garb that don't draw no attention." He nodded to Monk. "Go through the trunks in the hold. See what you can find that'll serve the purpose."

"Yes, sir, Mr. Coop." Monk turned to leave.

"And see about some boots. Them moccasins ain't fit for this kind of weather."

"Yes, sir, Mr. Coop," Monk called over his shoulder.

"But first," Matt announced, "I've got to get across the bay." When Captain Coop frowned, Matt explained. "I left some personal items over there."

Coop looked at Monk. "You up to some rowing, Monk?"

"Ready as ever, Mr. Coop."

Leaving well before sunup next morning, the two

reached Boliver Peninsula mid-morning. Two hours later, Matt had recovered his gold and they pushed off for Galveston Island. At ten o'clock that night, they pulled up to the *Tahiti Tradewind.*

Chapter Twenty-five

The next week, Monk accompanied Matt to Houston, the two hitching a ride on a stern-wheeler puffing up Buffalo Bayou into the heart of the city.

His face covered with a month-old beard, Matt wore woollen trousers and matching coat, a homespun linen shirt, and a Confederate greatcoat. On his hip rode a ball and cap pistol, a present from Cooper.

Despite the rigors and deprivations of reconstruction on Southerners and the chilling January mists, carriages and wagons of every description packed the streets, the sidewalks bustled with men and women heading in every direction, and businesses buzzed with new commerce.

Monk had done a good job selecting clothing for Matt. No one gave him a second glance. While Monk waited outside, Matt entered the offices of the Oriental Clipper Lines to inquire about the departure of the next ship bound for Shanghai, China. The harried clerk informed him that the ship, the *Ivory Clipper,* would depart in two weeks and there were still a few passages available.

"Now," Matt said to Monk outside the office, "all I have to do is find Carson."

Monk chuckled. "That's not as simple as it looks, Mr. Matt."

The wiry cowpoke, the skin drawn even more taut over his face after the last weeks recuperating, laughed with him. "I can't argue that, Monk." He extended his hand. "Best you get on back. Tell Coop if I get the chance, I'll stop by before I leave. If not, I'm much obliged."

Nodding slowly, the massive black man asked, "What do you plan on doing now?"

Matt shrugged. "Same thing as before. Hit every saloon I can. Carson can't stay out of them. If I don't find him, then I'll catch him when he boards."

"What if he figures on boarding in Galveston?"

Matt's eyes twinkled. "Don't forget. I'm taking the ship down to Galveston. If I don't find him here, I'll find him there."

"Yes, sir. That the ways to do it."

As he watched Monk disappear into the bustling crowds filling the sidewalks, Matt's smile faded. He didn't feel as confident as he led Monk to believe. In fact, he told himself, he could probably find a single speck of gold in all the sand on Galveston Beach before he could find Ed Carson.

But he had no choice.

He purchased a new Colt .44 that he strapped to his right hip after moving the ball and cap to the left. A fifteen-inch Bowie completed his arsenal, all hidden beneath his heavy coat.

For the next week, he scoured the seedy bars and dangerous saloons, remembering the recent attempt on his life.

To his dismay, he saw no sign of Carson.

A week before the *Ivory Clipper* sailed, Matt booked passage, an inside cabin so as not to call attention to himself. Two days before departure, he went aboard, learning upon discreet inquiry he was the first to do so.

For the next two days, sitting at the window of an upscale tavern, he watched passengers board, searching for the giveaway height and bulk of Carson.

To his consternation, the big man failed to put in an appearance before the schooner set sail for Galveston.

Matt stood at the rail, staring gloomily down Buffalo Bayou as the topsail schooner made its way slowly downriver. What if Carson had changed his mind? What if at this very moment, he was heading across the state?

From where the *Ivory Clipper* docked that night, Matt could see Captain Coop's schooner, the *Tahiti Tradewind,* moored at the docks just north of Sixth Street.

For a moment, he considered paying the old gent a visit but decided instead to spend his time waiting for Carson to put in an appearance.

The night was long and cold but Matt persevered.

No Carson.

Early next morning, a few hours before the clipper's departure at sunrise, Carson still had not arrived. Matt stared at the empty loading dock, muttering a soft curse and wondering what had happened to the big man.

Then he spotted a bandy-legged little man in a black suit and captain's cap hurrying through the patches of lamplight to the *Ivory Clipper.* He recognized Cooper Williams. The small man spotted Matt and waved him ashore.

On the dock, Matt grinned. "Captain Coop. It's good—"

"No time for that." He grabbed Matt's arm. "I think Monk's found this Carson gent you been looking for. He's dressed fancy like, but he's got that scar over his right eye. One shaped like an arrowhead. Hurry."

Matt cast a glance back at the clipper. "But—"

"You got time. But, if this is that Carson jasper, he ain't got much time. Fact is, he might be facedown in the bay right now." The smaller man scurried across the docks, heading down one of the hundreds of dark alleyways of the old city. "If this is the feller you been looking for, he's got hisself in trouble with a gang of wharf-rats who follow a piece of scum called One-Eye Jack." Coop turned onto a cobblestone street. "I don't know what he done, but he's holed up in a sugar warehouse on the docks."

The dim gaslamps along the narrow street glittered off the sheen of mist clinging to the soft brick walls of the warehouses lining Campeche Street.

Ahead, a dark figure emerged from the shadows of the warehouse. Monk hurried to meet them. He nodded to the brick walls. "In there. He calls hisself Joe Higgins."

Matt's pulse raced. *Higgins! Pink's last name.* "You sure? Higgins?"

Monk nodded. "He buy passage to Shanghai on the *Ivory Clipper,* but there are those who will stop him."

"You mean, kill him?"

Monk nodded.

Matt's eyes narrowed. Maybe, he told himself, he should just step back and let someone else do the job for him. Either way, Carson would be dead. Still, he reminded himself, there was the gold Carson and his band had stolen from the wagon train. It seemed only fitting that those who survived were entitled to the money. He studied the dark building. "Where is he?"

Monk nodded to the three-story brick building. "In the sugar loft—third landing."

Matt frowned at the large black man. "Doing what?"

"Waiting. There be five cutthroats inside. They wait for One-Eye Jack."

"Where is this One-Eye Jack hombre?"

Monk shrugged. "All I knows is, he's a-coming."

Matt realized that whatever he planned to do, he had no time to waste. That Jack jasper could show up at any moment. Shucking his greatcoat, Matt slipped the Bowie from its sheath.

Monk grunted. "I go with you."

Matt stayed him with his free hand. "No. You and Captain Coop live here. I don't."

Coop snorted. "That don't make no difference."

"Maybe not now, but a year, five years from now—besides, call it a favor for me."

Reluctantly, Coop and Monk agreed, and Matt ducked inside the dark building and froze in the shadows, giving his eyes time to adjust to the dark. When he shifted his feet, he heard the crunch of dirt and sand under his hard leather soles. Quickly, he slipped from them, preferring the silence of his stockinged feet.

Lanterns hung throughout the cavernous building, marking stairs and passageways. He peered into the gloom hanging over the first flight of stairs, studying the shadows surrounding them. Then his eye caught movement. Someone was crouching at the base of the stairs leading up to the first of three cantilevered landings jutting from the east wall of the warehouse.

Swinging wide around the jasper at the stairs, Matt took advantage of the stacks of sugar arranged in neat rows, ready to be hauled out and loaded on the next ship.

As his ears grew accustomed to the sounds of the warehouse, he picked up the scratching of rats' feet as the creatures skittered through the darkness.

A faint groan sounded above the faint whispering of the rats. Then directly in front of him a dark figure rose, stretched his arms over his head, and yawned.

Silently, Matt palmed the blade of the Bowie and clubbed the cutthroat on his temple. The jasper collapsed like a sack of feed corn. Matt quickly bound and gagged him, then rolled him into the shadows.

Seconds later, he climbed the stairs.

As he reached the second landing, a voice to his right called out, "Call it off, Higgins. Give us the saddlebags, and you can walk out of here. You know what One-Eye Jack will do. He'll carve out your gizzard."

A familiar voice replied from the darkness of the third landing. "He does that, he'll never find the money."

Another voice joined in, this one not ten feet from Matt. "Don't make us laugh. You come in here with it. We'll get it if we have to tear the place apart."

"Tell you what," Carson shouted from the landing above, "I'll split with you."

Sarcastic laughter greeted his proposition.

He warned them, "I'm heeled. You got to come up them stairs. I'll kill every last one of you before you reach the top.

Laughter echoed through the warehouse again.

Matt took advantage of the laughter. Like a wraith, he floated through the shadows and cold-cocked a second cutthroat.

Off to his left, a voice called out, "Peck! You all right? What was that noise?"

In a gruff voice, Matt muttered, "Yeah!"

For a moment, the silence seemed to expand until it was ready to explode. Then the voice replied, "Oh."

Moving silently, Matt reached the rear of the second landing. He climbed onto the stacks of bagged sugar. Silently, he pulled himself up over the edge of the third landing and lay panting in the darkness. After he caught his breath, he looked around. He could not see more than a few inches, but he spotted a glow from outside. Easing forward, he extended his hand and touched a window. Next to the window was a row of bagged sugar stacked head high.

The slamming of a door echoed throughout the huge building. A voice called out, "Spanker!"

The voice that had been doing most of the palavering with Carson replied, "Up here."

Matt started crawling forward across the landing through the darkness toward the top of the stairs, the direction he surmised Carson was hiding. Ahead, someone cleared his throat.

Matt hesitated, squinting into the darkness before him, seeing nothing.

From below, One-Eye Jack bellowed, "Give it, Higgins. Nobody steals from me and lives to tell about it. Come on down, and I'll kill you fast. Otherwise, I'll make it slow, real slow."

Carson laughed, a braying sneer. "Come up here and you're a dead man. I got rifles and cartridges. Back away, Jack. You can't wait me out. Come morning, others will come in."

Moving silently, Matt slipped forward, but only for a few feet before his outstretched fingers touched the cold wood of a rifle butt. Tentatively, he ran his fingers up the stock until he touched a box of cartridges, then another rifle. Carson had an arsenal up here. Beside the rifle, Matt's fingers ran over a leather flap. He froze, recognizing the object as a pair of saddlebags.

"You hear me, Higgins?"

"Yeah. I hear you."

While the conversation was taking place, Matt's shaking fingers opened the flaps. Disappointment washed over him when he felt no gold coins, but then his fingers touched stacks of paper. Obviously, Carson had converted the gold to currency so it would be easier to carry.

He checked the other pouch. It too was packed with paper currency.

Fastening the flap back over the pouch, Matt eased backward. The loft was thick with dark shadows.

And then he had an idea, an extravagantly wild idea, but one that just might work.

Looping the saddlebags about his neck, he eased to the side of the window, then picked up one of the hundred-pound sacks of sugar. Into the darkness, he spoke, "Good-bye, Carson."

A shocked gasp was followed by the sound of a heavy body scooting around in the shadows. "Fields!"

"I've got the money." With that he hurled the bag through the window, ducked behind the stack of bags, then scampered over the edge of the third loft into the pitch-black shadows below.

Chapter Twenty-six

"Blast you, Fields!" A gunshot erupted from the darkness.

One-Eye Jack's voice echoed from the second landing. "Get up there, now."

More shots rang out as feet pounded up the flight of wooden stairs. The third level of the sugar warehouse echoed with curses and gunshots.

Carson groaned as two slugs slammed into his chest.

Hastily, Matt crept through the shadows to the edge of the second landing and lowered himself quietly over the side to the floor below. Quickly, he dropped down to the first landing. Near the door, he retrieved his coat and boots, slipping into them before slipping out the door.

Behind him, still bound, one of the cutthroats watched.

In the sugar loft, the dim glow of a lantern illuminated a stunned Carson sitting on the floor, slumped over, his head leaning against the wall, blood leaking from the wounds in his chest.

Jack kicked him viciously in the side.

Carson stirred.

"Wake him up," Jack ordered, his one good eye glaring malevolently at the semiconscious man.

Spanker heaved a bucket of water on Carson, who sputtered and tried to pull away.

Jack grabbed a handful of Carson's hair and shoved his head back. "Where's the money, Higgins?" He touched the point of a knife to Carson's throat.

Carson tried to turn his head to the window but Jack held tight. "Out there. Matt Fields. He took it and jumped out the window into the bay."

Shooting a glance at Spanker to check the bay below, Jack hissed, "You better not be lying to me."

From below came a cry. "Jack! Some jasper just run out the front door with the saddlebags."

Jack jerked his head at one of his men who immediately hurried to a window, spotting the indistinct figure on the docks three stories below. "He's down there, Jack."

Jack's eye narrowed. His fingers twisted Carson's greasy hair ever tighter. "Liar!" he said, driving the knife through Carson's throat.

Carson's eyes grew wide. He tried to scream but the only sound he heard was the blood gurgling in his throat.

Jack jerked the blade from Carson's throat, wiped the bloody blade on his grimy denims and nodded to Spanker who, with a cruel chuckle, rolled Carson out the window and into the bay below.

Matt headed for the livery at the east end of the docks. Once out of Galveston, he could circle the bay and cut north. A week would put him up in the thick forest with the others.

At the livery, he found a sound bay and a worn but well maintained center fire rig. He tied the saddlebags behind the cantle and fished the gold from his pockets to pay for the gear.

He clicked his tongue and rode out of the livery barn.

Instantly, he reined up.

Heading toward him was One-Eye Jack and his band of cutthroats. "You should have killed the two of them when you had the chance, Matt," he muttered.

To the east, an orange glow tinged the horizon.

Matt dismounted and tied his bay to the corral rail.

His blood ran cold as he moved out to face the men. "That's far enough, Jack."

The six jerked to a halt. One-Eye Jack sneered. "Give us the bags. You can ride out."

Matt took a step forward and rolled his shoulders. He had come too far to back away now. His eyes grew icy, his jaw firm. This time, he wasn't going to play fair. "Forget it. You want trouble then come ahead, but this money goes back to those it belongs to, not a bunch of greasy thieves." With his last word, his Colt leaped from the holster.

Jack's eye grew wide. "Why you—" He grabbed for his six-gun, but Matt's Colt was already blazing.

A crushing blow like a sledgehammer hit Jack in the chest, staggering him back into his men who were firing frantically.

Matt felt a slug tug at his wool coat, and another brush his thigh. His Colt continued to roar, spitting out pain and death. When the hammer clicked on a spent cartridge, Matt holstered the revolver and shucked his ball and cap.

Four men lay on the ground. Two more were running for the wharves. His hammer cocked, Matt eased forward. Jack lay staring with lifeless eyes at the sky that was growing lighter every moment. The other three were rolling about moaning and clutching at their bellies.

Moving among them, Matt kicked their revolvers

away. Behind him, he heard footsteps. He spun, but it was just the old liveryman hurrying to see the commotion. Matt handed him two double eagle gold pieces. "Bury them."

Without another word, he climbed back into the saddle and rode out of Galveston.

That night, Matt opened the saddlebags. He whistled as he counted out sixteen thousand in federal currency. "So that's what Jack was after."

In addition to the gold Carson had taken from the wagon train, he'd stolen another ten from One-Eye Jack.

He closed the bags and studied them. They were filled with blood money, all except six thousand. Of course, he reminded himself, sixteen thousand—no, eighteen counting his and Cotton's—would start up a right handsome ranch, one big enough for him and the boys and Charley, and most of all, Mary Elizabeth.

Still, his and Cotton's own two thousand would give them a right good start. And if the boys and Mary Elizabeth decided to pitch in, they could build themselves a fine spread, maybe one of the largest in the state some day.

Two days later on the way back to the northern forests of Texas, he spent a night as a guest of an order of Catholic nuns in central Texas. After he left the next morning, the novice whose duty was to clean the rooms fainted when she discovered ten thousand dollars on the bunk with a note thanking them for the night's hospitality.